WISHING UPON A CHRISTMAS STAR

Book VIII of The Seven Curses of London Series

LANA WILLIAMS

A Victorian Romance Novella

Copyright © 2018 by Lana Williams

All rights reserved.

By payment of required fees, you have been granted the *non*-exclusive, *non*-transferable right to access and read the text of this book. No part of this text may be reproduced, transmitted, downloaded, decompiled, reverse engineered, or stored in or introduced into any information storage and retrieval system, in any form or by any means, whether electronic or mechanical, now known or hereinafter invented without the express written permission of copyright owner.

Please Note

The reverse engineering, uploading, and/or distributing of this book via the internet or via any other means without the permission of the copyright owner is illegal and punishable by law. Please purchase only authorized electronic editions, and do not participate in or encourage electronic piracy of copyrighted materials. Your support of the author's rights is appreciated

No part of this book may be reproduced or transmitted in any form or by any electronic or mechanical means, including photocopying, recording or by any information storage and retrieval system, without the written permission of the publisher, except where permitted by law.

Thank you.

Cover Art by The Killion Group

Other Books in The Seven Curses of London Series:

TRUSTING THE WOLFE, a novella, Book .5
LOVING THE HAWKE, Book 1
CHARMING THE SCHOLAR, Book 2
RESCUING THE EARL, Book 3
DANCING UNDER THE MISTLETOE, Book 4, a Novella
TEMPTING THE SCOUNDREL, Book 5, a Novella
FALLING FOR THE VISCOUNT, Book 6
DARING THE DUKE, Book 7,

Want to make sure you know when my next book is released? Sign up for my newsletter.

Chapter One

Bombay, India 1871

Baxter Adley stepped onto the terrace of a bungalow in Bombay, needing a moment away from the party he attended. His nose twitched at the warm night air that was filled with exotic fragrances. Would his English senses ever grow accustomed to the sights, sounds, and humidity of this country even after living here for nearly three years?

Thoughts of home pulled at him more and more frequently of late. Was it some instinct that called him back? Or merely a morose mood brought about by the idea of once again spending Christmas so far away from England. November would soon be here, and that had him thinking of the holidays, despite the lack of anything resembling mistletoe or snow in India.

With a sigh, he set aside his glass of gin and leaned against the wrought-iron railing that lined the terrace to study the night sky. A banyan tree with its wide-reaching roots and impressive canopy blocked part of his view. Though he reminded himself that if he were in London, the stars would no doubt be covered by soot and clouds, it didn't stop the ache in his chest at the thought of his mother and father and all else familiar that he'd left behind. Unfortunately, life as he'd known it in England no longer existed, stolen by a professional thief who'd convinced his elderly father to invest in a "fool-proof" plan.

His parents had moved to a more modest residence shortly after his departure, his father determined to reduce expenses after the poor decision that nearly ruined them. Hence Baxter's venture to India. As their only child, it was his responsibility to return financial stability to the family.

Trading tea, cotton, and gemstones along with a few other select items had proven lucrative. Diversity was key. Never again would one poor choice put his family's income at risk, even when presented by a schemer intent on tricking others. Worst of all, the ruse had stolen his father's confidence and zest for life. He no longer trusted himself to make investment decisions or any others, it seemed. Baxter hoped that would return with time, and that his own accomplishments—along with the money he sent each month—gave his parents some measure of security along with happiness.

While Baxter received letters from home, it was impossible to read between the lines to know their true status. His father had been so dispirited and his mother little better when he'd left. Were they truly enjoying life despite their reduced circumstances? He certainly hoped so.

The two to three-week journey between the countries discouraged trips home. In truth, he worried a visit to London would tempt him to remain there, bringing an end to his business. He intended to move back eventually, but not until he'd refilled the coffers to the extent that his parents wouldn't have to worry ever again.

These years on foreign shores had forced him to determine who he was without the trappings of wealth. He didn't know how he'd fit in when he returned to London as a businessman instead of part of the aristocracy. Though his father would probably never hold a title as the third son, their previous family wealth had held open many doors. The funds Baxter had earned didn't compare.

The uncertainty of his own future caused him to be in no hurry to return to London, despite missing his parents. Besides, going home meant the possibility of another rejected suit from a prospective bride. He'd fancied himself in love with Lady Alice Hayes and thought the feeling mutual. But word of his changed circumstances had spread like fire, and she'd quickly snuffed his budding feelings, leaving him with no doubt that *he* was not enough without money. The pain of that moment still stung.

Surely this longing for family and home would soon pass. He could blame the feeling on the gin. His current life might be lonely and filled with financial interests rather than personal connections, but he preferred it that way. Keeping business his priority instead of pleasure allowed him to send a substantial portion of his profit home for his mother and father, an ability that filled him with pride and satisfaction.

He'd suggested his parents find a larger home in his last letter, but they insisted they had all they needed in their current residence. The idea of them once again living comfortably—if modestly compared to their former life—brought a smile to his lips, something that was a rarity these days.

For now, his days were filled with purpose, which gave him a certain amount of contentment. Happiness would have to wait.

He shook his head, aware he should be inside, making more of the connections that earned him business, not alone on the terrace with thoughts of home and Christmas.

With a long, slow breath, he braced himself against the longing and attempted to stuff it deep inside where it normally remained buried. Where he needed it to stay, so he could focus on increasing his business.

Yet his eyes betrayed him and wandered upward. An unusually bright star above the horizon caught his notice.

And held it.

The pure beauty of it stole his breath, much like a brilliant crystal gemstone he'd recently traded. His mother would call it a Christmas star, an omen of how wonderful the holiday would be, and a reminder of the reason for the celebration.

"I wish," he whispered, yet he couldn't bring himself to finish. Doing so out loud would release that longing, and he feared he couldn't bury it again. Instead, he closed his eyes and finished the wish silently, unable not to.

For a life as big and bright and as full of hope and joy as the star.

Scoffing at his wayward thoughts, he opened his eyes, unsurprised to find nothing had changed. He reached for his drink and reminded himself he hadn't expected anything. Life was much simpler when expectations were minimal.

He glanced one last time at the Christmas star and returned inside, determined to forget it. After all, hope and joy were luxuries he could still not afford.

LONDON, ENGLAND

MISS VIOLET FAIRCHILD PLACED A FINGER ON HER bedroom windowpane and traced a path around the unusually bright star visible in the crisp October sky.

"I wish..." She paused, hesitating to finish the thought.

The brightness of the star suggested it held a special power. She didn't want to waste a wish like that on something trivial.

What *did* she want?

With a sigh, she realized she wasn't quite sure. On the one hand, she had nothing about which to complain. She had a roof over her head, plenty of food to eat, and a warm bed in which to rest. As she'd learned of late, not everyone in London had those things that only a few years ago, she'd taken for granted.

Yet a certain restlessness filled her. Did she wish for happiness? How could she when she wasn't certain why true joy eluded her? Nor was she unhappy. Perhaps a better word was discontent.

She'd seen this restlessness in her older sisters. Each of them had solved the problem by finding a purpose, claiming a cause. Why did the thought of doing so form a knot in the pit of her stomach?

Though alike in appearance with blonde hair and blue eyes, she was different than her sisters on the inside, where it counted. She had a terrible flaw that she detested, and she'd found no way to overcome it—a lack of courage.

The realization had come to her when her eldest sister, Lettie, had first become involved with a cause. Violet had been appalled to hear the details of her sister's treks into the East End and what she'd done.

Her other sisters, Rose and Dalia, had followed in Lettie's footsteps in their own ways. Each had been rewarded for their efforts and found not only a purpose but the love of an amazing man.

Logic followed that if Violet wanted the same things in her life, she needed to find a way to help others less fortunate. A difficult task when the thought felt so overwhelming.

The East End was the most obvious place to offer assistance. But it was also an intimidating area, filled with people who lived in an entirely different version of London than she did. Desperation was a living, breathing entity there, and she didn't know how to navigate it.

All she knew was that she was ready for more in her life. Helping others was the obvious way to fulfill that need.

But how?

She studied the star more closely, hoping for an answer. Hoping for the right words to make her wish the best and brightest one, just like the star.

Her breath caught as it came to her.

"I wish for something new and meaningful in my life."

Somehow, those words felt just right, filling her with hope and anticipation.

Chapter Two

Violet smiled with satisfaction at the embroidery piece on which she worked. The festive holly design on the handkerchief was quite striking and would make an excellent gift for one of her four sisters for Christmas.

While her parents didn't do much to celebrate the holiday, Violet thoroughly enjoyed it. Christmas Day meant a festive meal, often held at one of her sister's homes, along with the exchange of gifts. She promised herself that when she had a family of her own, she'd make a true celebration of the season and begin her own traditions.

"Why do you think Mr. and Mrs. Adley next door don't have more servants?" asked Holly, her younger sister by three years.

Violet looked up from her needlework to see Holly nibbling on a biscuit and peering out the window. Again. "A better question might be why you insist on spying on the neighbors."

Holly loved nothing more than a good mystery. Whether she found it within the pages of a book or in the world around her mattered little. The problem was that she often invented them.

"I'm not spying." She frowned at Violet over her shoulder. "Mother insists I restrain from such behavior. I prefer to think of it as taking an interest in the wellbeing of our neighborhood."

"Hmm." Violet raised a brow, wondering if Holly truly believed her own excuse. All the same, Violet couldn't resist setting aside her needlework to join Holly at the window.

She'd noticed more and more signs of decreased circumstances next door as well. The older couple had moved in nearly three years ago, but they'd seen less of them as time passed. The Adleys rarely attended gatherings anymore. The paint along the windows of their home was peeling. Their gardens were in desperate need of pruning, but nothing had been done to halt the overgrowth.

"I wonder if their funds have become tight," Violet said.

"I thought the reason they moved here from their previous home was that they'd fallen on difficult times."

Violet had heard that as well, but she didn't confirm the rumor as she didn't want to encourage Holly to share the information with others. Violet preferred to think of herself as above gossip, though she was as curious as her sister.

"What if they've become so pressed for money that they're starving at this very moment?" Holly glanced at the biscuit she held in her hand. "Perhaps we should bring them some of the cook's treats. We could spare a cake or two."

"I hardly think anyone living in this neighborhood is so poor as to be unable to buy food." But as Violet stared at the house, she realized it showed a definite lack of maintenance, more so than she'd previously noticed. Could there truly be a problem?

The idea of venturing next door with a basket of treats intrigued her. She'd met the couple on several occasions, and they seemed nice enough. In truth, she'd been longing to help those less fortunate. However, she hadn't managed to find the courage to go to the East End to locate someone in need, as her sisters had.

Lettie, the eldest, had surprised her family by insisting on helping neglected children. That mission had taken her into several inappropriate places near the East End.

Rose, the next in line, had caught the eye of a duke and now did some charitable work as part of her position as a duchess, though Violet didn't think she'd ever ridden through the East End in her carriage, let alone stepped foot there.

Dalia had saved their maid from certain disaster by convincing her not to become a fallen woman, which had placed her in danger on more than one occasion.

Luckily, their parents hadn't realized her sisters' activities until they were over. Violet doubted they knew to this day just what Lettie or Dalia had done.

Violet had concluded that she was simply not as brave as her sisters. This lack bothered her more than she cared to admit, and she was determined to remedy the situation.

In truth, she was surrounded by brave women. Her cousin, Sophia, had confronted danger when she'd played a part in saving the Royal Albert Hall from anarchists. Even her friend, Lillian, had found the fortitude to visit some seedy apothecary shops to track down an unsavory character placing additives in alcohol with poisonous side effects.

What had she, Violet, done? Nothing. Not one thing.

The lack vexed her and left her feeling like a failure. It wasn't as if she could purchase courage at a local shop. She'd tried researching the topic in several books, but they hadn't helped in the least. She still had no nerve for action of that sort. Somehow, she had to find a way to change that.

She'd even read *The Seven Curses of London* cover to cover twice over, but no ideas on how or who to aid had come to mind. At least, not any that didn't place her in danger. The book shared the author's view of the seven worst problems facing London. Her sisters had found answers and ideas within the pages but reading the details the author shared kept Violet up at night with images of starving children begging for money and professional thieves ready to pounce on her.

Could the small act of aiding the neighbors help her learn to be brave? Not all of those in need lived in the East End.

"What are you thinking?" Holly asked, eyes narrowed as she studied her.

"Nothing." If she decided to do this, she needed to do it on her own. Bringing Holly along would be cheating. She couldn't use her sister as a crutch for courage.

"Holly?" Their mother entered the drawing room, reticule in hand. "Are you coming with me to the milliner's?"

"I suppose." Holly didn't care for shopping, but she enjoyed new things and already had good taste in fashion, assuming their mother didn't manage to influence her overmuch.

"Would you care to join us, Violet?" her mother asked.

"No, thank you." She pointed toward her embroidery. "I'm going to continue with my needlework."

Her mother glanced at the piece, giving a nod of approval. "Your stitches are nice and even. Holly, did you see how lovely her stitches are?"

"Yes, Mother," Holly said with a scowl at Violet. She disliked needlework. "They're very good. Shouldn't we be going?"

Violet hid a smile at Holly's attempt to avoid a lecture on how she should spend less time reading and more time pursuing the attributes of a lady, a favorite lecture of their mother's.

Luckily, Violet didn't receive that particular lecture as she enjoyed needlework, drawing, and shopping, unlike her sisters. She feared that had something to do with her lack of courage. Could the two possibly be tied together?

As the voices of Holly and her mother faded in the foyer, Violet turned to look out the window again. Would bringing the older couple a basket of food insult them? Heaven knew her mother would be appalled if one of the neighbors brought them such a gift.

The garden door on the side of the house opened, and Mrs. Adley stepped out, a lovely Indian shawl draped over her shoulders. The day was a mild autumn one, making it a fine day to stroll in the garden.

Following her impulse, Violet rushed upstairs to fetch her cloak. Within moments, she stepped out of the rear door that led to the garden, which faced the Adleys'. Perhaps she could start a casual conversation with the woman, and an idea of how to proceed would evolve from there.

She slowed her steps as she turned at the box hedge that marked the beginning of the side garden, forcing herself to pause as though admiring some of the pink cyclamens that yet bloomed low to the ground. Thank heavens Holly wasn't there to witness her behavior.

Out of the corner of her eye, she could see Mrs. Adley hadn't ventured far and now stood staring at something. Violet edged closer but only saw a few dead dahlias. Why would she study those?

Violet cleared her throat. "Good afternoon, Mrs. Adley."

Startled, the woman turned to look at Violet. "Oh. Lovely day, isn't it?" Mrs. Adley was an attractive woman near Violet's height with green eyes and dark hair. She'd aged well, with only a few lines marking the area around her eyes, but she walked with a pronounced limp and often used a cane as she did at the moment.

"Indeed." Violet took her greeting as permission to

approach the wrought-iron fence that bordered their gardens. "I hope the day finds you well."

"Well enough, I suppose." A despondent note laced the woman's response, her smile much dimmer than her usual bright one.

"I don't mean to be forward, but may I ask if anything is amiss?"

To Violet's shock, the woman reached up to wipe a tear from the corner of her eye.

"May I join you, Mrs. Adley?" Violet asked, anxious to help or, at the very least, offer comfort.

"Of course. So kind of you. I don't know what's come over me," the woman managed between sniffs as she sank onto a bench and propped her cane beside her.

Violet hurried to the rear of their garden and stepped out to walk quickly to the Adleys' garden entrance. The gate didn't appear to be locked, but she couldn't open it. After much tugging and pulling, it finally swung free.

Mrs. Adley watched her struggle with dismay. "Not even the gate works properly." She shook her head, wiping at another tear.

"Just a bit rusted. Nothing that can't be easily remedied." Violet joined Mrs. Adley on the bench and handed her a handkerchief.

The woman sniffed as she took it. But rather than bringing it to her nose, she examined the embroidered design. "Oh, isn't this lovely." She looked up at Violet, her green eyes glittering with tears. "Did you embroider this?"

"Thank you. Yes. I enjoy needlework." She couldn't help the defensive note in her tone as her sisters tended to berate her for the feminine pursuits she enjoyed.

Mrs. Adley nodded and at last used it to dab her eyes. "I'm sorry to be so weepy."

"Is there anything I can do to aid you?"

Mrs. Adley reached over to pat Violet's arm. "So kind of you. Please forgive me, but I don't remember which of the Fairchild daughters you are."

"Violet." She waved a hand in the air to dismiss the older woman's concern. "No need for an apology. Four of us look very much alike. You're not alone in your confusion."

"Violet." The woman nodded. "Of course."

Violet looked away to give her a moment to collect herself. The garden was in an even worse state up close. What had once been lovely flower beds amongst neatly trimmed hedges now had a neglected, rather wild appearance.

"It's a mess, isn't it? I don't know why it's upsetting me so much today, but I can't seem to help myself."

Violet bit her lip, uncertain how to continue. While she didn't want to pry, she couldn't offer assistance if she didn't know more. "Did you lose your gardener?"

"Yes and no."

With a frown, Violet turned back to the woman. Had she not heard Violet's question or was far more than the garden losing its edge?

Mrs. Adley sighed. "I shall tell you a secret if you promise not to share it."

"Of course." She was very good at keeping secrets.

"We haven't had a gardener since we moved here. Our butler has done his best to keep up on things, bless his heart. But he suffers from stiff knees, which have grown worse the past year. Poor Watsford is growing older right along with Mr. Adley and me. I've told him not to bother with the garden. I miss it though. Its current state only reminds me of how things used to be." She blinked rapidly and made use of the handkerchief again.

"There's nothing wrong with the garden. It's merely in a more natural state." Violet looked around, trying to believe her own reassurance. "You might be starting a new trend with its appearance."

Mrs. Adley rewarded her efforts with a smile. "You are a dear, Miss Fairchild. I shall try to think of it like that as well."

Violet bit her lip as she considered how best to phrase her next question. She wanted to help but didn't want to insult her. "Can I assist in some way?"

"Good heavens, no." She waved the handkerchief. "All is well. I suppose it's just the coming holidays that have me so melancholy."

"Oh?" Violet didn't know quite what to say but couldn't resist reaching out to pat the woman's arm.

"Christmas isn't what it used to be."

"Tell me," she said, using the one skill she knew she had—the ability to listen.

※

BAXTER RETURNED HOME AFTER A LONG, DIFFICULT DAY AT his office near the docks. Delayed shipments and ridiculous excuses set amid a cultural difference that was a challenge to overcome were normal. However, his patience to deal with it was lacking.

He poured himself a drink, appreciating the peaceful quiet of his library. The servants were accustomed to his need for solitude after his workday and left him alone. He sat at his desk to review the personal correspondence he'd ignored the past two days while resolving the issues at his office.

The elegant cursive on an envelope caught his eye. He withdrew it from the stack, a smile forming when he saw it was a letter from his mother.

He quickly broke the wax seal, anxious for word from home. His mother's feminine, if precise script, greeted him.

Dearest Baxter,

We hope this letter finds you well.

His smile broadened as every letter she sent opened with that sentence. The routine sentiment warmed him.

She shared random bits and pieces of news. His father was enjoying the mild weather they were having. She'd ventured to Bond Street with friends. He hoped she'd been shopping as it was one of her favorite past times. She'd refused to purchase anything for a long time after the reversal of their financial circumstances. It had taken some convincing on his part that she could resume. But for the past year, she often mentioned afternoons on Bond Street in her letters.

We've met the most delightful young lady. She's coming to mean so much to your father and me and has been helping us in many ways.

He frowned at the paragraph as he reread it. Helping? How, he wondered.

We're coming to rely on her more each day. She has wonderful ideas for us.

Alarm bells sounded as Baxter read further. The last time they'd relied on someone, the man had convinced his father to invest in a precarious scheme that had cost him his fortune.

Even more telling was that not once did his mother inquire when he would make the trip home. She asked that in every letter. But not this one and the holidays were approaching. That was a telling detail in itself. The past two Christmases, she'd employed every technique a mother had in her arsenal—suggesting, asking, demanding, and finally, the strongest one of all, guilt.

He'd nearly given in last year at her reminder that they weren't getting any younger and who knew how many more holidays they'd live to see.

Of course, he wanted to return home. The opening of the Suez Canal had shortened the trip by over five thousand miles, but it was still a lengthy one of at least two weeks, often more. Part of him feared that if he went home, he wouldn't have the strength to return to Bombay, which would bring his business to an end. He wasn't ready to set aside the substantial stream of income the business brought. Not yet.

He read the letter again, trying to interpret what was truly happening with his parents. No matter how many times he studied the words, the alarm bells wouldn't be silenced.

Baxter stepped over to the bell pull and yanked the cord.

"You rang?" Rajesh, his valet, asked from the doorway a few minutes later.

"Please make inquiries as to when the next ship is traveling to London and pack my bags. I'm returning to England for a time."

"Of course, sir. How long do you intend to remain there?"

Baxter considered the question, uncertain. "Three weeks at most."

"Will you be staying there for the English holiday?" he asked.

The idea tempted Baxter more than he cared to admit. However, doing so would only make it more difficult to return to Bombay. Once he saw to his parents' well being, he needed to come back to India, regardless of the date on the calendar.

"I don't know." Yet he couldn't prevent the anticipation that filled him at the possibility.

Chapter Three

"Do be careful, Watsford," Violet said as she watched the butler step onto the lowest rung of the ladder in the Adleys' foyer.

The dust and cobwebs on the massive crystal chandelier had been bothering Mrs. Adley though they never lit it anymore, so Violet wanted to help clean it. However, she didn't care for the way the elderly servant tottered then paused to find his balance. That would never do.

He insisted his bad knees had improved, but she had her doubts. She'd suggested she should be the one to climb the ladder. After all, she was the youngest person in their home, but Watsford refused her offer. She knew if she insisted he'd be insulted. He didn't care to be reminded of his advancing years or his bad knees.

"I can see from this angle that we'll need a different candle. Do you suppose you have one somewhere?" She bit her lip, hoping he wouldn't see through the ruse.

"Of course, miss," he said and stepped down, much to her relief. "I'll return shortly."

"No need to hurry," she said as she eyed the chandelier. Though it should be lowered to be cleaned, the fixture was heavy. With no strapping footman to aid them, Violet had thought the safest option was to climb up to it rather than risk dropping it.

Mr. and Mrs. Adley were the kindest, gentlest souls she'd had the good fortune to meet. If anyone deserved a little help, it was them. As long as her mother didn't find out what sort of assistance Violet was providing, all would be well. She thought Violet came over to the neighbor's home to read to them.

That had been how her visits had started over four weeks ago and was something she still did. The older couple took turns picking the books. Mrs. Adley had chosen a lovely collection of poems they'd all enjoyed. Mr. Adley had decided on one on Greek history the first time, but his latest selection had been a delightful mystery that had kept them guessing to the end.

It hadn't taken more than one visit for Violet to realize how short-staffed their home was. She had delicately inquired as to why they didn't have more than Watsford and his wife, who served as housekeeper and cook, along with a day maid who came three times a week.

Their lack of funds was an uncomfortable topic, especially for Mr. Adley, who blamed himself for their misfortune. Violet had quickly brushed aside the discussion so as not to upset him.

She had spent the last several weeks helping with a few small projects around the house and garden, but her main task was providing encouragement and a little direction. Whenever Mrs. Adley mentioned something she wished could be done, Violet did her best to make it so. She'd tidied the drawing room on one of her visits, given them several of her embroidered pieces to make into pillows, and helped Watsford clean the windows. She could do little with the worn carpets or slightly tattered wingback chairs, but the drawing room was bright and cheerful despite that. She and Mrs. Adley had even made a bit of progress in the garden when the weather permitted, though now that December was upon them, warm days were rare.

More important than any of that was providing friendship, which she received in return. She'd even requested they address her by her given name soon after her visits had started. The couple had slowly withdrawn from Society over the past few years and never received callers. They'd lost much of their enjoyment in life. She hoped her three to four visits each week, no matter how brief, had helped to give it back.

As soon as Watsford disappeared at the end of the hall, Violet reached for the damp cloth and stepped onto the ladder herself. After all, she'd climbed the ladder in her father's library numerous times. This should be quite simple.

However, five steps up, she realized it felt different. The ladder wobbled precariously, causing her to catch her breath. She slowed her progress and took the next few steps with care, staying centered on the rungs.

Another step and she reached the chandelier. A glance below caused her heart to thud dully. With nothing to hold onto other than the top of the ladder or the chandelier, she felt terribly unsteady. She swallowed back her nerves and lifted the cloth to rub one of the crystal pendants. To her dismay, she needed both hands to keep the pendant from swinging, so she could clean it.

The front door bell rang, a rare event from what she'd experienced. The sound startled her, and she reached for the ladder to catch herself. She knew Mr. Adley had been on one his rambles, as he liked to call his long walks. The door opened, but she didn't dare take her eyes off her task to see his reaction to her standing on the ladder. He wouldn't be pleased.

When he didn't say a word, she risked a glance out of the corner of her eye.

But it wasn't Mr. Adley standing there. Instead, a handsome stranger frowned up at her. One who was broad of shoulder with sun-kissed skin, and the most arresting green eyes she'd ever seen staring up at her.

"Whatever are you doing?" His deep voice rattled her with its timbre.

"I—" She gasped before she managed another word. The ladder tipped precariously as she shifted. To her horror, the ladder moved one way, and she went the other.

BAXTER'S HEART FLEW TO HIS THROAT AT THE SIGHT OF THE falling woman. Without a second thought, he rushed forward, arms outstretched, and caught her.

The attractive young woman had blonde hair and lovely blue eyes that had gone wide with the near miss. "You startled me."

"That makes two of us," he said, still cradling her tight against his chest. "Are you all right?"

"Who are you?" she asked as she blinked up at him, bringing long lashes to his notice.

"I believe I should be the one asking that question." He hadn't slept well on the fifteen-day journey from Bombay to London, but his present confusion couldn't be blamed solely on his tiredness.

The state of the exterior of the home in which his parents

lived was nothing like he expected. The house was in desperate need of a fresh coat of paint. The steps required repair. And the garden was more of a jungle than those in Bombay. Where had the money he'd sent each month gone?

The lady in his arms suddenly pushed against him as though only now realizing he still held her. He set her on her feet, keeping his hands on her slender waist to make certain she had her balance.

Her cheeks were a lovely shade of pink, complementing her creamy skin. Her hair was drawn back into a loose chignon with a few wisps near her ears. A black rim encircled the blue of her eyes, giving them an exotic appearance. Blue eyes were a rare sight in India, and he found himself staring into hers with fascination.

"Who *are* you?" he repeated, suddenly desperate to know.

She stepped back, removing his hands from her waist, making him realize he still held her. Her cheeks flushed an even deeper shade as she drew back another step, one brow raised. "I belong here. The question is, who are you?"

Stubborn thing. Beautiful, but stubborn. She smelled of violets. Intelligence glittered in her eyes. His senses were inundated by everything about her.

"Baxter Adley," he managed at last.

The mix of reactions that crossed her face amused him. Shock. Denial. Curiosity. Awareness.

Damn if he didn't feel all those too. He gave himself a mental shake. Surely his reaction was only due to his exhaustion, not because he appreciated the way she felt in his arms. He reached for the ladder and set it upright as he glanced at the chandelier. "You do know there's a rope to lower that."

She lifted her chin, folding her arms before her, obviously displeased with his remark.

Ah, he thought. She didn't like to be questioned. That

made him want to do so again, just to see the spark in her eyes.

"I'm well aware of that. However, it's quite heavy."

"Why wouldn't the footman assist you?"

Her lips pursed into a bow that shot an arrow of awareness straight through him. He had to glance away in response. What on earth was wrong with him?

"What relation are you to Mr. and Mrs. Adley?" she asked.

He risked looking back at her, surprised. She couldn't have been acquainted with them long if she didn't know that. Or was something else afoot? "Their son."

Those lips parted as her gaze swept over him from head to foot and back. "Truly?"

He frowned, unable to make sense of her question. Was she the person his mother had mentioned in her last letter?

"Mr. Baxter?" He turned to see Watsford entering the foyer, a candle in hand and a wide smile on his face.

Baxter's world settled slightly as he strode forward to clasp the butler's hand and shoulder. "Good to see you, Watsford."

"And you as well, sir. We weren't expecting you." His voice held a slight note of reproach.

"I wanted to surprise Mother and Father. Are they in?"

"Your mother is." Before Watsford could say more, the drawing room door opened, revealing his mother.

"Did I hear something fall?" she asked, cane in hand, before her gaze landed on him.

Baxter's heart squeezed at the sight of her, a rush of love coming over him. He shouldn't have stayed away so long.

"Baxter!" The delight that spread over her face made him smile. "Whatever are you doing here?" She dropped her cane to spread her arms wide to embrace him.

"Mother." Everything else fell away as he held her tight.

She felt frailer somehow, a dimmer shade of her previous self. But he'd worry over that later. The tight band around his chest loosened for the first time since he'd received her last letter. His relief at finding her well took precedence over all else.

"Let me look at you," she said and leaned back, putting her hands on his cheeks to frame his face. "Baxter." Tears sparkled in eyes a paler green than his own as she studied him. "You've been gone too long."

Her close inspection allowed him to do one of his own. Fine lines that hadn't been there before tugged at him. He hated the idea of her aging. "You look as beautiful as always." That much he knew beyond a doubt.

The sound of a quickly indrawn breath reminded him of the young lady's presence.

"And you are a dear," his mother said as she released him. She took his hand and turned him toward the woman. "Allow me to introduce Miss Violet Fairchild. She's been assisting us with…a few things of late."

Of course her name was Violet, the same fragrance she wore. "Oh?" He was quite curious as to what those things might be.

"She lives next door and has been such a blessing since we've come to know her."

Guilt reared its ugly head, but he tamped it down as best he could. He was pleased his mother and father had companionship of some sort. Why the young woman had been attempting to clean the chandelier was a question he'd ask later.

Miss Fairchild dipped into a curtsy as he bowed.

"Fairchild?" he asked, as the name brought forth a memory. "I believe I had the pleasure of being introduced your sister prior to my departure."

23

"...d, perhaps."

"...believe so." This Fairchild was much different in ...pearance than the lady he'd met. "Thank you for seeing over my parents."

She smiled slightly and gave a nod. "My pleasure. They're a true delight."

"A delight?" He couldn't help but question the term. While he loved them, he also knew his father. Had things changed so much in the time he'd been gone?

"Watsford, will you bring in tea?" his mother asked.

"Of course, ma'am." He smiled broadly at Baxter again. "So good to have you home." He hurried down the hall, candle still in hand, to see to his mother's request.

"How long will you be in town?" his mother asked as he retrieved her cane. She led the way to the drawing room, her limp from a riding accident in her youth still noticeable. She paused before he could answer to look back at Miss Fairchild. "Do join us, my dear."

"I'll be there in a moment," she said, her smile forced.

He raised a brow as he glanced at her, wondering if she intended to finish her attempt to clean the chandelier. The urge to forbid her from doing so crossed his mind, but he resisted.

A lovely blush rose up her cheeks as if she'd read his thoughts. For some reason, the idea almost made him smile.

"Where's Father?" Baxter asked.

"On one of his rambles."

His father had been taking long walks in the afternoon for as long as Baxter could remember, regardless of whether they were living in the countryside or the depths of London. He called it his "thinking time."

"What has brought you to London?" His mother sat on one side of the settee, patting the place beside her.

"To see you and Father, of course."

Her eyes narrowed. "Why don't I believe you?"

"What other reason could there be?"

"A business matter, no doubt." She waited as though expecting a confession.

"Not at all. I realized when I received your last letter how much I wanted to see you." He decided now was not the time to mention his concerns. Certainly not while Miss Fairchild was listening.

"You're only here for a visit?" his mother asked.

"Yes." He could see how much his answer disappointed her. Had she expected him to say he'd decided to move back to London?

Before he could say more, Watsford carried in a tea tray. Miss Fairchild was directly behind him.

Baxter stood, using the distraction of Watsford's arrival to have a word with Miss Fairchild. "Done cleaning?" he asked with a hint of a smile.

She lifted her chin ever so slightly and met his gaze. "Now that you're here, there's no need for *me* to do it."

He frowned, wondering at her answer. Her pluck was admirable, but where was the footman to do such tasks? His gaze swept the room and noticed not all was as it should be. A worn rug covered the floor. The drapes were faded from the sun but had not been replaced. His mother had always kept their home in excellent condition. Was the current state a reflection of her no longer noticing such details or something else? Even his mother's dress looked far from new.

"Violet, would you be so kind as to pour?"

Baxter hid his surprise at the familiar form of address, a sign that Miss Fairchild must've spent a significant amount of time with his parents to be so welcomed here. He watched as she sat in the chair before the low table and reached for the teapot. The modest plate of sandwiches and biscuits were a shadow of what they'd been in his youth. But he couldn't make anything of that when he hadn't told them he was coming.

The butler stepped close to Baxter. "Mrs. Watsford asked me to pass on her pleasure that you're home."

"Please give her my best. I look forward to seeing her soon."

The butler nodded and stepped out of the room.

Before Baxter could retake a seat, his father's voice sounded from the doorway.

"You're not having tea without me, are you?"

He turned, wondering how his father would react to his presence. He'd noticeably aged as well, but Baxter hoped worry no longer caused the lines. His hair was more gray than black. His gaze caught on Baxter and the joy that lit his eyes caused Baxter to grin.

"Son!"

Baxter met him part way. His father grasped his shoulders, his gaze searching. For what, Baxter didn't know.

"How delightful that you've come." His father's smile warmed him.

"It's so good to see you."

Baxter's departure had been necessary as far as he was concerned, but his father hadn't agreed. His guilt over being taken in by the scheme had changed him, shaking his belief in himself and humanity.

Baxter's determination to find a way to recoup the loss had created an unexpected rift between them rather than reassuring his father as he'd wanted. He hoped the money he sent home showed both his parents how much he cared.

His father turned to his mother. "Isn't this wonderful?"

She beamed. "Wonderful, indeed."

His father's gaze caught on Violet. "Did you meet Miss Fairchild? She's become a dear friend to us."

Baxter nodded, trying to reconcile the man he'd left with

the smiling man standing before him. The differences were many. He hoped his father had forgiven himself for the drastic change in their lives. In his own eyes, there had never been anything to forgive.

Did Baxter have Miss Fairchild to thank for both the warm reception and the acceptance in his father's expression?

Chapter Four

Violet listened and watched with curiosity as she sipped her tea. While she knew Mr. and Mrs. Adley had a son as they'd spoken of him a few times, his arrival had been a complete surprise. Apparently, his parents had been equally as shocked as she was.

Baxter's handsome appearance made her think of foreign shores with his tanned skin and unusual jade green eyes. His dark hair and strong build made him impossible to ignore. Being cradled in his arms had been an experience she couldn't describe, nor would she soon forget.

The thought of those brief moments sent her pulse fluttering even now. She'd never reacted to a man like that, but then again, she'd never been held like that either. Surely her fright was the reason for the lingering dancing sensation in her stomach.

What caught her notice even more than the way he looked was his obvious affection for his parents. That melted her heart. Yet there was an unmistakable watchfulness between Baxter and his father. Perhaps her sister, Holly, was wearing off on her as she wondered at the cause of the undercurrents of tension running between them.

"How are things in Bombay?" Mr. Adley asked as Violet refilled their cups.

Heat filled her cheeks as she poured for Baxter. Good heavens. She'd blushed more since his arrival than she had in the past year.

"Busy." His deep voice rumbled through her, causing her to tremble slightly. "Still lucrative, though challenging at times."

"Do you enjoy living there?" Violet asked. She couldn't imagine living somewhere so different from London. Nor a place so far away from everything familiar.

Those arresting green eyes shifted to her, and she felt as if he still held her. She caught her breath, teapot in midair.

"Parts of it are enjoyable. The weather is quite different than in London."

"The plant life you've written to us about must be something special to see," Mrs. Adley said, causing Baxter's attention to move away from Violet.

She gratefully drew a breath and set down the pot before she spilled it.

"Indeed, it is. The flowers are unique, as are their scents," Baxter continued.

Spicy? Sweet? Violet would've liked to ask, but the idea of drawing his attention back to her was more than she was prepared for at the moment.

Mr. Adley watched Baxter as he spoke, a look on his face Violet couldn't interpret. Though obviously pleased at Baxter's presence, it almost seemed as if he had something he wanted to say but couldn't bring himself to do so.

Mrs. Adley's expression spoke of her happiness at her son's return. Three years was a long time to go without seeing family.

What had caused him to stay away for that length of time? She knew the trip would be a long one, even with the opening of the Suez Canal. What had lured him to Bombay to begin with?

His fine wool jacket and trousers fit him well and spoke of financial success. She dearly wanted to know what business he was in but didn't want to ask. Instead, she settled for observing.

Baxter's gaze lingered over the room, as though he didn't find things quite as he expected. She hoped he saw that his parents needed some assistance and intended to remain in London long enough to help.

When a lull in the conversation filled the air, Violet asked the one question to which she dearly wanted to know the answer. "How long will you be staying?"

That green gaze fastened on her once again. "I haven't yet determined that."

"I do hope you'll stay through the holidays," his mother said as she reached out to pat his arm. The stark longing in her expression was more than Violet could bear.

"That would make the season very special," Violet added, hoping to convince him to agree.

"A Christmas to remember," Mr. Adley said in a quiet voice as he watched his son, his expression unreadable.

"Do you remember what fun we used to have during the holidays?" Mrs. Adley asked, glancing between her husband and Baxter. "Ice skating. Snapdragon. Caroling. Kisses under the mistletoe." The memories lit her face.

"Was it Elliott, your cousin, who fell through the ice at the Miller's pond?" Mr. Adley asked Baxter. "His clothes were nearly frozen by the time we fetched him out of the water."

"Oh!" Mrs. Adley's eyes went wide as she laughed. "I'd forgotten that."

"I was quite young at the time. Perhaps only ten years of

age. I thought him mad for venturing onto the ice when you told him not to," Baxter added with a smile as well.

"We gathered greenery every year with other families no matter how cold it was." Mr. Adley rubbed his hands together as though remembering the chill all too well.

"Remember when Molly, the Talbot's eldest daughter, burnt the tablecloth because she didn't know how to play snapdragon but wouldn't admit it?" Mrs. Adley asked with a shake of her head.

"She nearly set the drapes on fire," Baxter added, grinning.

Mr. Adley's chuckle made Violet want to join in. She'd never seen the pair so animated. Baxter's presence obviously brought forth many good memories.

"And the dancing." Mrs. Adley sighed with delight. "Such a lovely time."

"We could do all that again." The words escaped Violet's lips before she could stop them. Yet how could she not make the suggestion when the older couple's eyes sparkled with such happiness at their memories?

That sparkle faded as Mrs. Adley shared a long look with her husband as if she knew such a celebration wasn't possible. She waved her hand to dismiss the idea. "No need for that. Ignore me. I just enjoy thinking of those times."

"Of course we can," Violet insisted, shifting to the edge of her chair. While she knew their funds were tight, the activities Mrs. Adley mentioned weren't expensive. They only required a bit of planning.

Mr. and Mrs. Adley seemed to remain unconvinced based on the doubtful look they shared. However, neither did they refuse the idea outright.

"Couldn't we?" Violet turned to Baxter with a pointed stare. He'd been gone nearly three years. The least he could do was stay for Christmas and help to make it a special one for his parents.

His expression was unreadable as he met her gaze. She raised a brow, wondering if he'd dare refuse.

Baxter could only blink at the pointed stare Miss Fairchild leveled at him. He'd nearly forgotten the stories his parents shared. His memories were of the elaborate balls they'd hosted and with far too much food and drink.

What was it about the attractive young lady that brought forth his parents' longing to relive the past? Whether he was weary from the long trip to London or something else, he couldn't quite wrap his thoughts around what was happening.

The happy memories had removed years from his father's expression as well as the tension Baxter had sensed. And the hope in his mother's eyes was enough to make Baxter clear his throat to push back the emotions that threatened to overtake him.

Still he hesitated. Staying home for Christmas seemed a terrible idea despite his initial pleasure at the thought before he'd left India fifteen days ago. Somewhere, deep inside, he feared that if he did so, he wouldn't be able to force himself to return to Bombay. He'd promised himself to reach a significant level of revenues before he moved back to London. Enough that they wouldn't have to worry about losing all they had ever again. While he was nearing the amount, another two or three years of work were critical. Operating the business from London would be nearly impossible.

Returning home also meant facing the future rather than living in the limbo in which he'd existed for so long now. That limbo had kept him from having to make decisions and plans for the years ahead—something he wasn't prepared to do. Not yet. Staying here meant venturing into Society again, which would bring him face to face with the question of who he was now and how he fit in, as well as the possibility of having to face his past mistake. He preferred to avoid those issues until he was clearer on what he wanted.

"Couldn't we?" Miss Fairchild repeated, her expectant expression demanding he agree.

He couldn't understand why she was doing this or what was in it for her. What was she about? While he couldn't imagine that she intended to harm his parents in any way, financially or emotionally, he needed to be sure. Doing so required he remain in London for a time.

He also intended to discover where the funds he'd been sending had gone, for his parents were clearly not spending any on themselves. Questioning that while Miss Fairchild was here seemed a poor idea. He didn't want to say anything that would embarrass his parents.

"Of course," he said at last, his mind reeling. What had he just agreed to? It felt like far more than simply soaking some raisins in brandy, so they might play a silly game that tended to burn one's fingers.

Yet the approval that swept through Miss Fairchild's eyes had him returning her smile. Since when did a stranger's approval have any effect on him?

She clapped her hands, her smile one of genuine pleasure. The same heat that had come over him when he'd caught her in the foyer filled him as she held his gaze. Her obvious delight made his chest feel tight and uncomfortable.

"Wonderful." Miss Fairchild released the spell she'd cast on him when she looked at his mother and father. "You must tell us everything. I don't know that we can promise ice skating, but what other things did you do?"

His mother sighed, a smile still on her lips. "A kissing bough and greenery. A Yule log."

Miss Fairchild looked at him again. "Will you help me to remember all this or should I write it down?"

He could hardly remember his name when she looked at him like that, let alone a list of things. The mix of expectations and joy in her expression was something he didn't think he could live up to. Neither did he have it within him to say no.

"I shall do my best to remember." What madness was this? He'd returned to London for a completely different purpose other than to celebrate Christmas.

Miss Fairchild positively beamed in response.

Who was she and what was going on here? It was in that very moment that he knew he was in serious trouble.

Chapter Five

Baxter tapped on the library door before opening it the next morning, hoping to have a moment alone with his father. Though he'd had time with his parents after Miss Fairchild left the previous afternoon, he hadn't wanted to ruin their high spirits with talk of money or the lack thereof. It felt wrong to stroll in after being gone three years and question his father about everything from the paint to the furnishings to their clothing. He told himself he wanted to have a good night's sleep before broaching the uncomfortable topic and had retired early.

Unfortunately, he was still reluctant to speak of it. The last thing he wanted was to offend his father or wound his pride. But the starkness of the guest room in which he'd slept insisted questions be asked.

Sure enough, his father sat at his desk chair, staring out the window that overlooked the side garden. For a moment, Baxter didn't think he'd heard the knock.

Then his father turned, no surprise in his expression at the sight of Baxter in the doorway, only pleasure. But the tension he'd sensed the previous day had returned.

"Good morning, Baxter." His father rose and gestured toward the window. "I was just admiring the fine December day."

Baxter's chest tightened at what he was certain was a lie. Did his father think it necessary to pretend all was well? Baxter hated the thought. They'd always enjoyed a good and honest relationship.

Until the day his father had delivered the terrible news.

That day was one Baxter had relived countless times. It had changed them both. The stricken look upon his father's face was something Baxter hoped never to see again.

The realization that their entire fortune had disappeared without a trace along with one Horace Tisdale, the supposed barrister who'd presented an investment 'guaranteed' to pay a significant return, had been shocking.

Baxter realized that life as he'd known it had ended, that the plans he'd made were no longer possible. His carefree days of time with friends, parties, and horses had come to an abrupt end. Much of what they owned would need to be sold to pay creditors. Their accounts at various shops, including the tailor, would be closed. Even his horse, a bay he'd recently purchased and grown fond of, had to be sold. He'd been forced to grow up quickly.

His father's honesty at that moment had only made Baxter respect him more. He hadn't held back the truth but admitted to being taken in by the smooth-talking barrister who'd convinced both his father and his man of business that the mining venture in Brazil he proposed was foolproof. The man had presented evidence that previous investments in the mine had resulted in massive profits. Evidence they later realized had been forged.

Baxter knew his father wasn't greedy. He'd only hoped to provide for his family and future heirs in a way that would change their lives for the better.

Instead, those hopes had not only been dashed but stomped on.

Another blow was yet to come for Baxter. He'd been on the verge of proposing to Lady Alice Hayes, who was everything he thought he wanted in a wife—attractive, titled, and with similar interests.

Before Baxter could tell her the unfortunate news, she advised him that she'd already heard. He'd expected her to tell him such things didn't matter. That she loved him, and the news changed nothing. Instead, she'd looked at him as if he were beneath her now that he had hardly a shilling to his name.

That rejection had hurt far more than the news his father had shared. It had also made him determined never to be without money again. He'd lost his friends, his social standing, and the woman he thought to marry in a matter of days. Seeing Alice on the arm of another man—a wealthy one—convinced him that he'd narrowly escaped what would've been an unhappy marriage, but it was still a situation he never wanted to repeat.

"Father," Baxter began, trying to determine which of his many questions to ask first and how to do so without causing offense.

His father offered a small smile. "So good to have you here, Baxter. We've missed you."

"I've missed you as well."

"Do you truly intend to remain through the holidays? If not, tell me now before your mother's hopes rise too high."

Baxter's throat pinched. He'd been gone far too long if his father doubted his word. "I'd be pleased to stay for Christmas."

"But after that, you'll return to Bombay?"

"The business is doing well there." This was his chance. The opportunity to ask what in heaven's name his father had done with all the funds he'd sent. To ask why his parents were living in genteel poverty rather than in the manner to which he'd expected.

Yet he hesitated when his father's gaze fell to the desk, his finger tracing a pattern on the surface as his brow furrowed.

Baxter waited, certain he had something to say.

At last, his dark eyes met Baxter's as he opened a drawer, withdrew a sheet of paper, and slid it forward. "It's nearly all here. In an account in your name. I've taken only enough to pay for basic living expenses."

Baxter stared at the ledger, stunned by the size of the number at the end of the neat rows of entries.

"With this, you should be able to marry anyone of your choosing," his father added. "I'm proud of what you achieved in India, but you don't have to return there if you don't want to."

"No." Baxter was dismayed at the figures. "This was never what I intended. The money was for you and Mother."

His father shook his head. "I lost nearly everything with my foolhardiness. I don't deserve to spend what you've earned." His gaze lifted to meet Baxter's, his expression resolute. "I know exactly what you lost in the mess I created."

Baxter frowned. He hadn't told his father of Lady Alice's rejection as he feared it would only add to his guilt. Plus, the failure had been his as he'd chosen unwisely. He'd been so certain that she cared for him and money wouldn't matter. How naively stupid of him. He would never make that mistake again.

"I didn't lose what is most important." He came around the side of the desk to clasp his father's shoulder. "You and Mother are all that truly matter."

Moisture filled his father's eyes. "Son." He pulled Baxter into his embrace, and Baxter knew he was home at last.

Despite what his father had shared, Baxter intended to return to India, but before he left, he'd put things right at home. His parents deserved that and more. Surely, he and his father's difference in opinion regarding the funds could be resolved as long as they had this.

VIOLET HATED TO THINK OF HER VIGIL THE PAST TWO DAYS on the Adley household as spying, but how else could it be described? Watching for signs of Baxter or activity of any sort from inside her house was slowly driving her batty.

The undercurrents swirling in the drawing room upon his arrival had kept her firmly on this side of the garden fence. Surely the polite thing to do was to allow them time to reunite as a family.

But she dearly wanted to know what was happening.

Far from the determined heroine in one of Holly's mysteries, Violet observed from a safe distance, out of sight and no doubt out of mind.

Annoyed with her thoughts, she walked away only to rush back to the window when an unfamiliar sound came from outside. Her gaze swept the house.

And saw nothing.

She shook her head. She'd turned into some kind of voyeur since Baxter's arrival, watching and wondering from afar, unable to move on with her own life until she knew what was happening next door.

What did she hope to see? *Baxter*. The unbidden thought twisted her lips into a scowl. Not true, she reassured herself. He was the reason she'd kept her distance. The way he'd looked at her, questioning her presence, made her wonder the same. Her purpose had become less clear since his arrival.

She hadn't forgotten her promise to help plan a Christmas the Adleys would remember. Already she had a few ideas for what they could do that wouldn't be costly. Soon, she'd have to gather her courage and call upon the couple to see if they still wanted to proceed. Part of her hoped that when she did, Baxter wouldn't be there. Unfortunately, the other part hoped he would.

Movement out of the corner of her eye drew her notice. A horse and wagon entered the alley then disappeared. The fact that they didn't emerge farther down the alley meant they had to have stopped at the Adley residence.

With an excited gasp, she rushed out of the drawing room, slowed down in the hall so as not to attract the notice of any passing servant—or, heaven forbid, her mother—and entered the morning room, which was closer to the rear of the house. The windows there afforded a better view of the alley.

As she watched, workers hauled rolled up rugs, two chairs wrapped in cloth, and two other pieces of furniture into the residence. What did that mean? The items only made her more curious as to what was happening inside.

"Violet? Whatever are you doing?" her mother asked from the doorway.

Violet spun as guilt flooded her. Potential excuses for her position at the window flew through her mind, but she dismissed them as quickly as they came.

"Just noting our fine weather," she tried, wondering if the lie would satisfy her mother.

Her dubious look suggested it didn't. Her gaze swung around the room, landing on the needlework Violet had abandoned there over two days ago. "Did you finish your embroidery piece?"

"No." Violet realized she hadn't touched it since Baxter's arrival. What on earth was wrong with her?

"Why not?" her mother asked as she moved to pick it up and examine it.

"I don't have the correct shade of green to finish it." At least that wasn't a lie.

"What shade are you in need of?"

"Jade green with hints of gold." Her description brought to mind the exact shade she wanted. Like Baxter's eyes. The thought caused her to bite her lip. Oh dear. She was in worse shape than she'd realized. Yet she knew no other shade of thread would do. A rich green with hints of gold.

She couldn't help but press a hand to her stomach at the sudden flutters there.

"Shall we see if we can find some at the shop this afternoon?"

Violet turned back to the window, wondering what she'd miss if she left her post.

"Violet?" Her mother came to stand beside her to look out the window as well. "Oh. The Adleys are having new things delivered. Lovely. I do hope they hire someone to paint their house soon. The windowsills are positively dreadful."

Violet had no doubt the new items were Baxter's doing. But what did it mean?

What if the older couple didn't need her anymore? The thought saddened her more than she cared to admit.

"Yes, let's shop for that thread," she said to her mother. "Then I'll be able to finish this project and move on to the next."

"You're not going to wear that gown, are you?" Her mother stepped back to look her over from head to toe.

Violet knew she should be used to the criticism, but she'd received the full brunt of her mother's not-so-helpful comments since Dalia's marriage to Spencer a few months ago and was growing weary of it. "I'll change and be down shortly."

She gave one last glance out the window, but no further activity was apparent. Upon her return from shopping, she'd have to pay a call and see what was happening next door. She only hoped they hadn't abandoned the Christmas plans.

Chapter Six

Baxter watched as his mother moved from the new chairs to the bureau and back to walk across the large Persian rug now gracing the dining room, admiring each piece in turn.

"Are you certain, Baxter? These seem like too much."

"Not at all," he advised. He'd spent the past two days insisting his mother and father purchase a few new things to update the worn-out ones. His father would be most unhappy when the painters he'd hired arrived. Then again, he already was.

A smile lit her face. "These pieces look even better here than they did in the shop, don't you think?"

He couldn't have stopped his answering smile if he tried. Her delight made him happy. From what he could tell, the trips to Bond Street she'd mentioned in her letters had been a ruse. He had yet to convince his father that spending the money he'd sent wouldn't jeopardize their savings.

His father had become positively tight-fisted in Baxter's absence. He'd let the "unnecessary" servants go and cut their food purchases to nearly nil along with wine and spirits. How

Mrs. Watsford managed to feed the household with what little supplies she had was a mystery to Baxter. Now that the pantry had been filled, the housekeeper was busy baking and cooking to her heart's content.

While Baxter appreciated his father's efforts to keep down expenses, the time had come to make updates and repairs. He refused to allow his parents to remain living as they had, making do with next to nothing when it was in his power to make changes. All his calculations had assumed the money he'd sent had been spent. Yet his father refused to accept that.

Yesterday, he and Watsford had selected a new footman and a full-time maid with the help of Mrs. Watsford. The elderly couple had taken excellent care of his parents, but they were getting on in years and couldn't be expected to work so hard. The idea of Miss Fairchild on the ladder in the foyer again had Baxter giving a mental shudder. Such tasks held too much risk to be treated lightly.

His mother studied Baxter, a frown marring her brow. "But your father—"

"Will adjust," Baxter said firmly.

In truth, he had yet to convince his father that all would be well. The numbers on the ledger page were something his father had focused on increasing for some time. Each month when Baxter had sent money, he'd taken only enough to pay for the basic expenses. He refused to believe he deserved any more than that.

His mother stepped forward to run a hand along the gleaming surface of the bureau, her smile still in place. "I can't wait for Violet to see these things. She'll be delighted."

During the past two days, both his mother and father had referred to her in some manner more times than he could count. As if he had any chance of forgetting her. A glance out the window toward her residence had him wondering what she was doing. She hadn't called on them since the day of his arrival.

"I'm surprised she hasn't visited," his mother said. "We usually see her nearly every day."

Baxter had no doubt that was his fault. Her presence had unsettled him on several levels. He suspected she felt the same about him.

He hadn't known what to think from the way his mother had described Miss Fairchild in her letter. But he hadn't expected a beautiful young lady with blue eyes that closely studied him, making him feel as if he'd abandoned his mother and father.

He didn't know why it mattered what she thought of him, but it did. Perhaps now that she realized he cared for his parents and their wellbeing, they could forego the plan for a Christmas celebration. His mother hadn't brought it up since his arrival.

Christmas had lost its luster in the last three years. The holiday had nearly been upon them when their circumstances changed so drastically. Since then, he'd become far more jaded about the season. That had served him well in Bombay where he could easily avoid celebrating.

"I hope she comes by soon, so we can discuss plans for Christmas," his mother said. "I've thought of a few more traditions to incorporate."

Baxter smothered a groan at her words. He was surprised his father hadn't protested the idea. Perhaps he could speak to him about it to see if he truly wanted all the bother of the festivities they'd discussed.

"What is it, Baxter?"

He turned to see his mother studying him far too closely. Since he had no reason to suggest they not proceed with the Christmas plans, he could only attempt a disarming smile.

"Nothing. Why do you ask?" He kicked himself for asking

the latter. Of course, his mother noticed he was uncomfortable with the topic.

"You don't seem enthusiastic at the idea of having a special Christmas."

"I suppose I'd rather have a more intimate, family affair than a large party. I know that's selfish of me, but I came home to spend time with you and father."

Her smile broadened once again. "I confess that I feel the same."

Relief filled him. Now if he could only convince her to tell that to Miss Fairchild, all of this could be avoided.

"I would much rather do the activities I mentioned with our family. And Violet, of course, if she's available."

"Of course." The front bell rang, preventing him from saying anything more.

The new footman was on duty, and Baxter heard him answer. A moment later, the servant stood in the doorway. "Miss Violet Fairchild is inquiring as to whether you're receiving."

"Show her in, please," his mother said.

Before he had a chance to brace himself properly, the woman who had unsettled him so stood in the drawing room.

"I hope I'm not interrupting," she said, her gaze holding on Baxter's for a long moment.

"Not at all." His mother limped forward with both hands extended to take hers. "I'm so glad you've come. I was just thinking of you."

"Oh?" Again, her gaze flashed to his, the uncertainty in her expression surprising him.

"I couldn't wait to show you the new furnishings." His mother released one of her hands to gesture toward the items.

"How lovely," Miss Fairchild said as she moved forward

for a closer look, her enthusiasm genuine. "They're perfect in here."

His mother beamed.

Baxter was amused by how close the two women seemed, despite their age difference.

"What does Mr. Adley think of them?" Miss Fairchild asked.

"He hasn't yet seen them. I'll advise him that they've arrived." Before Baxter could offer to do so, she was gone, leaving him alone with Miss Fairchild.

"It's very kind of you to see to the new furnishings." Her gown was a pale blue and cream stripe with a modest bustle that emphasized her slim waist. The color brought out the blue of her eyes and the pink of her lips.

Suddenly, all he could think of was the way she'd felt in his arms. Of her scent that should've smelled ordinary but somehow was just perfect after all the exotic fragrances he'd encountered in India. She smelled like...home.

Unable to resist, he took several steps closer to see if he could catch the scent again.

Her head tipped back as he drew near, leaving the creamy expanse of her neck visible along with the pulse ticking in the dip between her collarbones. Ticking frantically.

He wrenched his gaze from that spot to see the same awareness in the blue depths of her eyes that he felt. He might not know what this spark between them was, but it seemed a shame to waste it.

Even as he reached out a hand to touch her cheek, the sound of his parents' voices echoed in the foyer. A quickly drawn breath as he dropped his hand was the only sound Miss Fairchild made. Was it one of regret?

"What do you think?" his mother asked.

Baxter turned in time to see her gaze swing from him to Miss Fairchild, a questioning expression on her face. He drew back to afford his father a better view of the new items and to give himself a moment to collect his thoughts. He couldn't blame any of what he felt on tiredness from traveling this time.

"Quite nice," his father said with a nod. But Baxter could tell from the tightness of his lips that he wasn't convinced they should've spent the money on the items.

Baxter wished he could find a way to reassure his father that all would be well. The success of the importing and exporting business he'd built surprised even Baxter. He'd found an excellent source for semi-precious gems, something highly desired in England and had made a sizable profit on them. The other goods he traded did well also. But the continued success required his presence in India.

Miss Fairchild glanced between him and his father as though sensing the tension. She walked forward to grasp his father's arm and draw him forward. "Come give the chairs a try."

To Baxter's surprise, his father did as requested, and they each sat in one.

"Very comfortable, don't you think, Mr. Adley?"

Her father reluctantly nodded as he ran his hands along the arms.

Baxter admired the way Violet coaxed his father into responding, even managing to gain a smile from him as he agreed that all the changes were good ones.

"Violet," his mother began, "I thought of a few more activities I'd like to include in our plans for Christmas."

"Lovely," she replied with a wary glance at Baxter. "I was wondering if we were proceeding with the idea."

"I would enjoy doing so. But we want to have just a family celebration with you included, Violet." His mother smiled at Baxter, a question in her eyes.

He couldn't help but frown. Since when did the plans depend on him?

"Shall we take a few minutes to discuss them?" Miss Fairchild tipped up her chin as if daring him to refuse.

※

VIOLET TAPPED THE PEN AGAINST HER LIPS, AS SHE SAT IN the Adleys' drawing room with Mrs. Adley the following afternoon. She had written down several of the older woman's suggestions but had yet to determine some of the details, especially where the best place would be to gather greenery. She wanted enough to decorate the drawing room, library, and dining room as well as a bough for the foyer table.

Her mother did very little in terms of decorating for Christmas, saying she didn't like the mess the fresh boughs made. Dripping sap could leave marks on the furniture, and dried needles created extra work for the servants, she insisted.

Violet was beginning to think it was a shame that her family didn't do more to enjoy the holiday, especially after hearing the stories Mr. and Mrs. Adley shared. The traditions they mentioned weren't costly or difficult, but they took effort and planning.

Violet had long been resigned to the fact that her mother only did such things if they benefited her or her daughters in some way. Or rather, if it would aid her daughters in making good matches. Whether her daughters enjoyed it was rarely of consequence.

Obtaining the greenery was a problem. It wasn't as if they were in the countryside where they could simply gather it. Finding it in London would be more difficult.

She knew Baxter was reluctant to help with these tasks, but she also believed he'd do anything to please his parents.

She had no choice but to use that knowledge to her advantage.

The greenery couldn't be brought into the house until Christmas Eve, as it was thought to bring bad luck if it was. But that meant she needed to know where to find some and how much to obtain before then, so it would be on hand.

"What has you thinking so hard?" Mrs. Adley asked from her new wingback chair as she flipped the pages of a book.

"Nothing." Violet didn't want to mention the issue as she knew the lady would suggest they forego gathering it. She disliked thinking she was inconveniencing anyone. Violet wouldn't allow that. Baxter was going to have to assist her with this issue whether he liked it or not.

She stared out the window for a long moment. "The gardens look much better, don't you think?" Everything was pruned and tidied for the winter. She knew how much their former disarray had bothered Mrs. Adley.

"Don't they, though?" the older woman agreed with a smile. "It will look grand by the spring. And did you notice the chandelier in the foyer?"

"I did, indeed. It positively sparkles now," Violet said before looking back outside. "Wouldn't it be a sight if it snowed on Christmas?"

"It rarely does, but that makes the few times it happens very special."

"Have you ever been ice skating when it was snowing?" The idea appealed to Violet. Big fluffy flakes creating a winter wonderland combined with the magic of gliding over the ice.

"Several times," Mrs. Adley replied with a smile. "If one is dressed properly, it can be quite romantic."

"And if one is with the right person?" Violet had to ask with a smile.

Mrs. Adley chuckled. "Even more enjoyable."

"What's enjoyable?" Baxter asked as he entered the room.

"Ice skating when it's snowing."

Thank heaven Mrs. Adley had answered as Violet couldn't bring herself to meet Baxter's gaze.

"Sounds like a chilly pastime."

Violet frowned at her list, certain she wouldn't feel the cold if she had the chance to do such a thing. She should've known Baxter wouldn't care to partake.

"Don't you think so, Miss Fairchild?"

"Please call me Violet."

He dipped his head in acknowledgement. "I'd be pleased if you addressed me by my given name."

"Very well," she said as she forced herself to look at him. "I think ice skating while it's snowing sounds wonderful."

"Humph."

Rather than argue the topic, Violet decided it best to change it. "Mrs. Adley, do you have a Yule Candle?"

"I don't believe so, though I can ask Mrs. Watsford to be certain." She set aside her book and reached for her cane. "I'll ask her now before I forget."

Violet watched in surprise as she rose and left the room, leaving her alone with Baxter. She drew a breath, determined to use this chance to ask him about some of the things she wasn't certain how to resolve herself.

"Do you know from whom we might obtain a piece of a Yule log to start ours?"

Baxter shook his head. "I can't say that I do."

"Do you know where we can gather evergreen boughs in the area?"

"No, I don't."

Violet sighed in frustration. "What part of the holiday do you intend to assist with?"

His gaze met hers, and she couldn't tell if those green depths held amusement or annoyance. "I confess I have yet to decide."

"Are you going to help at all?"

He scowled at her question. "In truth, I'm still questioning if it's necessary."

Ire filled Violet. "After hearing your mother and father share their memories, do you need to question that?"

"I have to wonder if the plans are for you or them."

Violet rose, needing to be on her feet to defend herself. "I can't believe you said that."

"Despite appearances, they have funds to enjoy whatever sort of Christmas they wish."

She'd seen the changes he'd made. Though she didn't understand the situation with their finances, she appreciated Baxter's efforts to improve his parents' lives. But that didn't mean they no longer needed this celebration, did it?

Baxter moved closer. "Why are you doing this for them?"

Violet eased back, shocked at the question. "Whatever do you mean?"

"Exactly what I'm saying. What are you about? What is your purpose?"

"To bring joy to your parents, of course." Yet his question sent her thoughts spinning. Could she say that when the things she'd done for them had been in part for herself? Had she been so intent on finding a cause that she'd created one where her help wasn't needed?

But she refused to admit any of that to him. She'd done her best to help them. The same was true for the Christmas celebration. If she benefited from it in some small way, what did it harm?

"For your parents," she repeated more firmly. "The question is what are you going to do to help make this another special Christmas they'll remember?"

Chapter Seven

Baxter strode through the front door that Samuel, the new footman, held open. "Does Miss Fairchild happen to be here?" After working with her throughout the past week, he no longer questioned her presence in his parents' home. Her visits fell nearly every afternoon of late.

"I believe she's in the drawing room, waiting for your mother to join her, sir."

He left his coat, hat, and gloves with the servant and entered the room, anxious to share his small bit of good news.

He might not understand her motivation for calling on his parents so often when she had her own family, but he appreciated her efforts to help all the same.

She'd assisted him in convincing his father that painting the house was necessary before the weather caused damage to the structure. She'd helped his mother select new fabric for the settee as well as a new chair for her sitting room, which had saved him from having to do so. Her enthusiasm for the changes made the tasks much easier for all of them.

Because of that, he'd put forth more of an effort to help with the plans for Christmas. It was the least he could do, considering what she'd done. He couldn't remember seeing his mother and father so happy in a long time. The more tasks he joined in for the planning of the celebration, the more memories came to the surface, though he was enjoying the new versions of them that Violet was creating.

"Violet?" he called as his gaze caught on her.

"You're just the person I need." She was standing on a bench, hands on the rod holding the drapes.

"What are you doing?" he asked as he hurried forward, fearing she'd lose her balance, much as she had upon his first day home.

"These aren't hanging properly. I was hoping to fix them before your mother did something drastic."

His mother continued to try to do things on her own rather than asking the new servants for help. She insisted they were busy with other duties and shouldn't be bothered with the small tasks she wanted to be done, though Violet wasn't any better.

"Allow me to do it instead." He drew close, holding his hands near her waist in case he needed to catch her.

The scent of violets that would now and forever make him think of her enveloped him, a lure he had to resist each time she was near. He tried to think of it as a warning that he was too close when he caught the fragrance. When he was next to her, he tended to think of things that had nothing to do with improving the house or preparations for the upcoming holiday.

But had everything to do with Violet.

He'd done his best to keep his distance. After all, he'd be returning to Bombay after the holidays and wasn't ready to consider a relationship at this point in his life.

"A moment, if you please," she said. "I nearly have it."

Yet the sight of her body swaying made his breath catch, leaving him no choice but to grasp her waist to steady her. She stiffened, making him all the more aware of their position.

Or perhaps of what he wanted their position to be.

He closed his eyes, trying to push the wayward thoughts from his mind but failing miserably. What was it about this woman that stirred his senses like no other?

She turned to put her hands on his shoulders, and he made the mistake of looking up at her to see the same awareness in her expression that he felt. That only made him want to take her in his arms and kiss her.

"Thank you." Her whispered words caused a pang of longing to shoot through him.

He forced himself to look up at the rod she'd been fixing. "Do you need me to do something?"

"I think I've done it." She removed her hands from his shoulders, but he couldn't make himself release her.

Instead, he lifted her off the bench to the floor. "You must take care. If something happens to you…" His train of thought vanished with the look in her eyes. For a moment, he would've sworn an invitation lingered in their depths.

His focus shifted to her lips. He wanted to know how she might taste. Did he dare find out? He had to try. He leaned close, testing her reaction, waiting for her to draw back.

But she didn't.

What was he to do but move closer still, tightening his hands on her narrow waist? Her lashes swept down to hide her eyes, but he was certain her mouth lifted the smallest amount. That was all the encouragement he needed to kiss her.

She tasted even better than he'd expected, her lips soft and warm beneath his. The sensations that flooded through him as though a dam had burst surprised him. He had to have more.

He hadn't felt anything like this in so long that he'd forgotten such things were possible. That alone was enough to make him think twice about what he was doing.

As though she felt his hesitation, she eased back, eyes wide with surprise as she put her fingers to her lips. Did that mean she'd felt the same spark he had?

"Oh."

Yes, he wanted to say. He understood every nuance she'd put in that simple word. *Oh, indeed*. His hands, still on her waist, tightened of their own accord.

"You were saying?" she asked as she tried to step back only to be halted by the bench on which she'd been standing.

He tamped back his desire with the reminder that he had no desire to court a woman, especially this one who challenged him at every turn. If he weren't careful, she'd be managing him as adeptly as she did his parents.

"You must take care for I fear my parents are quite set on their holiday, and it won't happen without you." He released her as he spoke, breaking the physical tether even as he forced himself to look away, needing to remove the visible connection as well.

"Of course." She turned her back to him to adjust the folds of the drapes.

Why did he have the feeling he'd disappointed her in some way?

"Did you need me for something?" she asked.

Though tempted to share just how much he needed her, admitting it would serve no purpose.

"I found someone with a chunk of a Yule Log who is willing to share it with us."

The delight in her expression as she faced him once again made him want to share news he knew would please her every day. She'd insisted not just any wood would do, that they had to have a piece from an actual Yule Log. She wanted to decorate the new log with holly and ivy then light it with the piece from a past one to cleanse the air from the previous year's events and to guard against evil. He was in favor of protection from both of those. The log would be burned each evening for the twelve days of Christmas.

"How wonderful," she said. "I'm sorry we didn't have any to share, but my mother doesn't like the mess of a Yule Log."

"Not all families do." His remark seemed to put her at ease.

"Can you imagine burning an entire tree as used to be the tradition?" She shook her head at the thought. "Imagine the risk of a fire."

"Other traditions hold less risk."

"It's rather silly of me, but I've always wanted to play snapdragon. I suppose because I read about it in a book."

"I've only played it a few times. Raisins that have been soaked in brandy are placed in a shallow bowl of brandy and the spirit is lit on fire. Quite an impressive sight in a dark room. The person who plucks the most from the flames and eats them wins. The trick is to be quick." He smiled, wishing he knew her thoughts. She seemed almost embarrassed by how little her family celebrated Christmas. "We'll soon find out if you will enjoy it as much as you hoped."

A genuine smile came to her lips. "I look forward to it."

Strangely enough, he found he was as well. The Twelve Days of Christmas were holding more and more appeal.

THE NEXT EVENING, VIOLET WAITED ON THE EDGE OF THE dance floor at the Morrison's ball for Lillian Bartley to arrive.

Her mother was already speaking with some of the other mothers.

Violet hoped her friend would provide the distraction she needed to enjoy the evening.

Violet hadn't had a moment's peace from her whirling emotions since her kiss with Baxter the previous day. Even now, her heart fluttered at the memory of it. Silly of her, she knew. It was only one kiss. Not even her first one, if she counted the time she'd been kissed last year by Andrew Crossing, a man she'd briefly fancied herself attracted to. The kiss with Andrew had convinced her otherwise.

She had to admit Baxter had provided her first *real* kiss. The kind that made one see stars.

And it had definitely caused her to see stars. Good heavens. Acting as if it had been of little note had not been easy. The problem was that she didn't want to feel this attraction to Baxter. He'd soon be leaving.

He'd turned her world upside down, unsettling her in every which way. She didn't like it one bit. In truth, she'd expected to have some sense of control over her feelings when she became attracted to someone. The realization that she didn't was unpleasant. Uncomfortable. Maddening.

"Why are you scowling at the dancers?" Lillian asked from her side. Lillian had arrived in London in the summer and was now engaged to the Duke of Burbridge. The love match was one to be envied, though Lillian insisted it hadn't begun that way.

"I'm doing nothing of the sort," Violet denied, only to realize she was still scowling. With effort, she forced a smile.

Lillian studied her, eyes narrowed. "Whatever has happened?"

"Why do you ask?" To her dismay, heat filled her cheeks.

"I don't believe I've seen a less sincere smile from you unless you're speaking of your mother. And now you're blushing. Something is afoot." She looped her arm through Violet's. Was it a gesture of support or a way to make certain she didn't escape before Lillian had found out more? "Do tell."

Now that she finally had a sympathetic ear, Violet couldn't bring herself to speak of the kiss.

"I'm waiting," Lillian prompted, making Violet realize she needed to share something to explain her odd mood.

"I'm helping to plan a special Christmas for the Adleys."

"The lovely couple who live next door to you?" Lillian had met them when Violet brought her over for a brief visit a few weeks earlier.

"Yes."

"What a wonderful idea. And such fun."

"It should be, except that their son has arrived home and is making the planning far more difficult."

Lillian's eyes went wide. "Baxter Adley?"

Now it was Violet's turn for surprise. "You know him?"

"No, but I heard Lady Alice speaking of him at the supper we both attended last evening." Lillian drew nearer. "She said they were quite close before he left for India three years ago and now that he's returned, she expects they'll renew their *acquaintance*." The emphasis Lillian placed on the last word made her meaning clear.

That information brought back Violet's scowl. "I can't say that I care for Lady Alice, nor do my sisters."

"She's not a nice person, but most men seem to ignore that as she's quite beautiful."

"Humph." Men were idiots not to see beneath her façade to her true self.

"Maybe we just don't know her that well," Lillian suggested.

Violet lifted a brow, not believing that for a moment. "I think she's revealed her true self to us because she's deemed us unworthy of being considered her competition. Burbridge doesn't look at anyone other than you."

"I do love that man." She glanced down at the beautiful engagement ring on her hand as though to remind herself he was hers.

"And he loves you. What exactly did Lady Alice say?"

"Nothing much more." Lillian studied Violet. "Why don't you set your sights on the mysterious Baxter? If nothing else, it would annoy Lady Alice to no end."

A denial died on Violet's lips as the man in question came into view and moved directly toward them.

"Good evening," Baxter said as he bowed, an amused glint in his eyes as though entertained by her surprise at his appearance.

Violet introduced him to Lillian, and they briefly exchanged pleasantries.

His regard returned to Violet. "Would you do me the honor of this dance?"

Violet didn't need to look at her friend to see her pleasure at the invitation. Now that Lillian was engaged, she seemed to think all her friends needed to find love as well.

"I'd be delighted," Violet said. And she was, no matter how much she told herself not to make too much of it.

He offered his elbow. Before she knew it, he'd swept her onto the dance floor, his hand warm and firm at her waist as the other held her hand for a waltz.

"Are you enjoying the evening?" he asked.

"Yes, and you?"

He didn't answer for a long moment as though debating his response. That only made her more curious as to what it would be.

"Some things in London never change." He sounded rather disappointed at the revelation.

"As in some *people* never change?" Was Lady Alice here,

she wondered. Had they had an encounter of some sort? She didn't care for the ache the notion brought.

"That is probably more apt." Then he shifted his focus to her, causing her to catch her breath. Something about his close regard made her feel as if the rest of the world fell away.

"You are a refreshing change," he said. Before she could ask what he meant, he added, "You look especially lovely this evening."

Her stomach dipped at his words, especially at the way his gaze lingered over her gown. The pale lavender wasn't a color she often wore as it made her think of her namesake, violets, and she'd been teased enough in her younger years to prefer to avoid the possibility. Choosing it as a fragrance was more subtle she hoped.

"Thank you. I didn't expect to see you here."

"I nearly didn't come, but a friend of mine convinced me to meet him here. How nice to find you in attendance as well."

He drew her closer as they turned on the dance floor. His moves were smooth and effortless, making her feel as if she were gliding instead of taking the required steps of the dance.

The result was lovely, and she couldn't help but smile. "You're an excellent dancer."

The corner of his mouth quirked upward. "She says with a touch of surprise."

She didn't bother to deny it when it was true. "Perhaps we should add dancing to the Christmas festivities we're planning for your mother and father."

His gaze caught on something past her shoulder. Something—or someone—who caused a darkness to shutter his expression. It was as if he'd stepped away from her even though he still held her in his arms. "You'll have to ask Mother."

If she hadn't come to know him so well in the past week,

she might not have noticed his sudden withdrawal. Was it in reference to the dancing suggestion or something else? Whatever caused it, she didn't care for the result.

Before she could discover anything more, the music swelled then drew to a close. He escorted her back to Lillian in silence, giving a curt "thank you" before moving behind her, quickly disappearing amid the other guests. Within a few moments, he stood speaking with Lady Alice.

Violet felt as if she'd been sampled only to be set aside for something better. Why had she thought for even a moment that she might be attracted to the man? She turned deliberately away, uncertain why his actions bothered her so much.

With effort, she searched for a topic to distract both herself and Lillian from Baxter's behavior. "Are your brother and his lovely wife here?"

"I do believe you're trying to evade answering my question," Lillian said.

"What question would that be?" Violet fought the urge to search the dance floor to see if Baxter and Alice were now dancing, telling herself she had no desire to know. She didn't want to see him look at Alice the way he'd looked at her.

"The one I asked prior to that dance," Lillian said, a sparkle in her eye that Violet didn't care for. "Why don't you set your sights on the mysterious Baxter Adley?"

Violet leveled her friend a glare that might've wilted a weaker friend but only made Lillian smile broader. "I wouldn't consider Baxter Adley as a potential suitor if he were the last man in London."

The clearing of a throat behind her made Violet realize she'd said the statement louder than she intended. A long moment passed before she realized it had been a male throat that had cleared.

No. Surely it couldn't be.

She quickly turned to face the eavesdropper to see Baxter

standing directly behind her. His gaze held hers for a long moment—long enough for her to realize he'd heard every word.

The frost in his green eyes speared straight into her heart.

Then he stalked away, exiting out the terrace door.

Chapter Eight

Violet sighed as she tried to focus on the Christmas dinner menu that Mrs. Adley had asked her to review. The holiday was only a week away, so she was once again in their drawing room.

But Baxter was not. He'd been out each time she'd visited his parents since he'd overheard her cruel comment. His absence had stolen any opportunity to apologize.

Two days had passed since the ball when she'd declared she wouldn't consider him as a suitor. Which had been a ridiculous thing to say since he hadn't asked to be or called upon her or sent her a token or flowers or...

She shook her head at the long list that clearly proved he wasn't interested in her.

Except for that kiss.

Oh, that kiss! The lilting sensation in her stomach had her drawing a long, slow breath at the memory.

If he hadn't annoyed her with his quicksilver change in moods while they'd danced coupled with his interest in Lady Alice, she wouldn't have said such a thing. She'd relived the terrible moment over and over. Though she didn't think she'd actually hurt his feelings as that wasn't within her power—was it?—she still regretted her words.

Sorely regretted them.

Wished she could take them back with every fiber of her being.

It was none of her business if he chose to renew his relationship with Alice. Never mind that kiss Violet and Baxter had shared. Did she think he deserved better? Yes. But some time in the middle of the night, she'd realized that if Alice was who he wanted, then maybe she would make him happy. He deserved to be happy. He was a good man who loved his mother and father and was doing all he could for them. That didn't mean Violet had to like his choice.

Mrs. Adley had said he was seeing to some business affairs. Was it true or was he avoiding her?

She brought her attention back to the menu, trying to think of something helpful she could add. "Does Mr. Adley like roasted goose?"

"Yes, though we haven't had it for an age."

"Where is he?" Violet asked, realizing she hadn't seen him for some time.

"He went on one of his rambles. He should be returning soon." A frown marred her brow, suggesting she thought he was overdue as well.

"I hope he comes back before the weather worsens." Violet rose to study the gray sky. A fine mist had started since her arrival at the Adleys' nearly an hour ago. A sheen coated the street. She couldn't help but shiver at the sight. "I wonder if it's freezing."

Mrs. Adley joined her at the window. "Oh dear." She studied the area, her look of concern evident. "I would've thought he'd return before it grew too treacherous."

Unease settled on Violet and refused to let go. "Should I go in search of him?"

The older woman paused for a long moment, as though considering her offer. "Let us give him a few more minutes before we worry. He hasn't been gone that long."

Violet reached out to gently squeeze her arm. "No doubt he'll arrive at any moment and admonish us for our concern."

Mrs. Adley gave a small smile, but it didn't reach her eyes. "I'm sure you're right." She turned back to the table where they'd been sitting. "Mrs. Watsford makes a delightful Twelfth Night pie."

Violet nodded as she moved back to stare at the list. "I look forward to sampling her recipe." The pie was made of chopped meat, dried fruit, sugar, and spices, some of which would be leftover from the Christmas feast. "Though I confess I've never eaten it all of the twelve days until Epiphany."

"But if you don't have some each day, you won't have twelve months of good luck."

"Hmm. I'm not sure if I believe in that particular tradition." The topic wasn't enough to distract her or Mrs. Adley from Mr. Adley's absence. Although only a few minutes had passed, Violet couldn't wait any longer. "Why don't I ask the footman to join me in searching?"

The sound of the front door closing had them both hurrying to the foyer only to find Baxter handing his hat and gloves to the footman. His black wool overcoat glistened with raindrops.

His gaze caught on them briefly before he turned his attention to unfastening his coat. "Is something amiss?"

"Your father has yet to return from his walk."

"That's not like him," Baxter said, holding his hand out for his things before the footman could set them aside. "He usually avoids walking in poor weather. Samuel, why don't you and I go in search of him?"

"I could ask a footman from my household to aid in the

search." Violet wanted some way to help as much as she wanted Baxter to forgive her. If only he'd look at her—

"With luck, we won't need him," Baxter replied, his gaze at last meeting hers, the flatness there making her regret her wish and causing her chest to tighten. "Samuel and I will have a quick look before we request more aid."

"Then I shall come too," Violet offered only to have Baxter raise a hand to halt her.

"Ice is forming on the street and walkways. 'Tis too dangerous."

Though she wanted to insist it was the least she could do, and how sorry she was about the other night, she said neither. "Perhaps if I kept to the grass—"

"Wait here," Baxter said as he donned his top hat, his tone brooking no argument.

The black hat made his eyes all the greener. Something about the sight made her want to step closer to adjust his overcoat so that it buttoned tightly about his neck. What was wrong with her?

With a last puzzled glance at her, no doubt because of the way she continued to stare, he and Samuel stepped to the door. "We'll return with him shortly. No need to worry, Mother. Perhaps you could request that Mrs. Watsford prepare tea. Something warm to drink will be most welcome for all of us upon our return."

"Of course." His mother limped down the hall to do as he suggested.

"Baxter," Violet pleaded, wanting to do something—anything—to help. And to apologize.

He only closed the door behind him and Samuel, leaving her alone in the foyer, feeling helpless.

BAXTER KNEW HIS FATHER'S NORMAL PATH WELL ENOUGH to direct Samuel to follow it, leaving Baxter to take the route in reverse. Surely, his father would've noted the deteriorating weather and be on his way home.

Each step required focus to avoid slipping as the mist froze underfoot. The temperature had dropped significantly, and a light breeze made the chill all the more noticeable. He told himself that at least it kept the image of Violet standing alone with a pleading look upon her face from his mind. Mostly.

With a sigh, he shook his head. Who was he trying to fool? He still couldn't remove the picture.

This wasn't the time to worry over her feelings. A new opportunity in his business had arisen, one he hadn't anticipated but could open many doors. He'd spent the past two days working through the details of it. But that hadn't kept him from thinking of Violet. He told himself over and over that he was pleased to have heard her say that she wouldn't consider him as a suitor. Nothing had been bruised but his pride. Mostly.

But the moment had proven that he wasn't prepared to risk rejection after all. Not when his emotions were in jeopardy. He hadn't intended to go to the ball, but when his friend insisted, he'd decided to test the waters and see if he still belonged or if he should remain out of Society for good. Attending hadn't been as uncomfortable as he'd expected. That is until Violet had stated her opinion so clearly.

He'd caught sight of Alice during his dance with Violet. Seeing her had shaken him. But not in the same way Violet did. He'd had to speak with Alice to confront what he felt as well to deal with his memories of the past. Her rejection had lived in him too long.

His feelings where she was concerned had been built up in his mind since he'd left London. He didn't want to take up with her where he'd left off but needed to determine what he felt. He'd been relieved to realize he didn't feel anything. Neither resentment nor affection. Nothing.

When he married in a few years, once he returned from Bombay, he intended to find someone who would provide the financial connections he needed to supplement their income. Yes, he thought with a nod. A business arrangement.

One that didn't have sparkling blue eyes or smell of her namesake.

Never mind the longing that rolled through him at the thought of Violet. Why was he tempted by her? His brief conversation with Alice should've served as a reminder of what could happen if one followed emotions rather than logic.

In truth, he should thank Violet for providing that reminder. Her declaration at the party had put an end to whatever simmered between them since his arrival. Christmas would soon be upon them, and then he'd leave all this behind. Mostly.

"Father?" he called, pausing to search the area, before repeating the process several times. He didn't pass anyone to ask if they'd seen him.

The farther he walked, slipping and sliding, the more he worried. Though he tended to think of his father as fit and healthy, he was growing older. He could've easily lost his balance in the freezing rain. Baxter nearly did several times. Thank goodness he hadn't allowed Violet to venture out in this weather. He didn't need two people to worry over.

The idea of his father falling and unable to regain his balance—or worse—kept him hurrying as quickly as he dared.

"Father?" he called again.

This time, he heard something. Heart thudding, he rounded the corner to find his father propped on an elbow on the walkway, his top hat on the ground beside him. Baxter's heart clutched at the sight.

"Father!"

"Good of you to come in search of me, my boy." The rough chuckle he gave wasn't its normal hearty sound, making Baxter even more concerned. "I lost my footing."

"Are you injured?"

"Only my pride, I think." He grimaced as he sat up and lifted one arm. "And perhaps my hand."

Baxter feared more than that was hurt as his father had yet to rise. With careful steps, he drew closer, realizing it was especially slippery beneath him.

"Why don't we shift you toward the street?" Baxter suggested, taking his father's uninjured arm to aid him. "Perhaps we can gain traction there."

"How good that you're home," his father said with a shiver as he slowly eased forward. "I'm not certain your mother would've found me."

"She and Watsford would've reached you one way or another," Baxter said, not liking his father's tremors. Nor the downtrodden way he spoke. "You know how determined Mother can be when she sets her mind to something. How long have you been here?" He studied the rosiness of the tip of his Father's nose and cheeks only to notice a bit of blood above one ear. "Did you strike your head?"

The puzzled look that crossed his face was concerning. Did he not remember? That sent worry pricking the pit of Baxter's stomach.

"I believe I may have struck the post when I fell." He glanced to one of the columns that linked the wrought-iron fence railings as he touched his head.

Thank heaven he hadn't struck one of the decorative points on the wrought iron, else he might not be speaking at all. The image brought a shiver to Baxter. Thinking of his father as fragile disturbed him.

He managed to ease them both to the street without falling then paused to consider his options, not willing to risk his father walking home. Before he could decide how to proceed, a hansom cab drew near. He raised his hand to catch the attention of the driver, only to realize it was pulling alongside them.

Violet opened the door and leaned out. "Would the pair of you care for a ride?" Her smile was forced as her gaze caught on his father.

"We would indeed," Baxter agreed, appreciating her effort at lightheartedness as much as the idea of a ride home.

"Take care," Baxter warned as she stepped onto the street.

The driver clambered down to assist them into the cab. "The horse has better footing on this stuff than us humans," he muttered. "Terrible weather we're havin' this day."

"We'll have you inside in no time." Violet's worried gaze met Baxter's as they helped his father into the cab.

Within minutes, they arrived at the house. Samuel had returned as well and helped him escort his father up the slick steps and inside with a concerned Watsford holding the door.

"Francis," his mother exclaimed. "Thank heavens. I've been so worried. Oh! You're bleeding!"

"Nothing to worry over," his father insisted. "Just a bit of a-a bump on the head when I-I lost my footing."

But Baxter could see that wasn't true. His father didn't seem able to put his weight on his right leg. "Watsford, ask the driver to fetch the doctor if you please."

The butler hurried to the door to call out to the man.

"Let us see you up to bed so that you can rest properly," Baxter suggested, hoping his father would agree. The man could be stubborn at the most inconvenient times.

"If you insist, though I'm perfectly well."

His father's agreement only made Baxter worry more.

"Excellent idea," his mother added. "Mrs. Watsford has a cup of hot tea ready for you."

"Have her add a shot of brandy to it." That sounded more like his father, Baxter thought.

Violet started up the stairs as he and Samuel assisted his father. Her gentle, encouraging words distracted his father as they half-carried him to his bedroom door. She opened the door wide and drew back the covers before stepping out.

He appreciated her help more than he could say. He and Samuel eased off his father's shoes and coat, then his jacket to make him more comfortable, taking care with his limbs.

They had him sitting up in bed when his mother brought in a damp rag to tend to his head while the maid followed with the tea tray.

Baxter stood aside, listening to his mother tsk-tsk over the injury to his father's head before rolling up his sleeve to take a closer look at his wrist. The bruise there was alarming and as difficult as it was for him to bend, Baxter wondered if he'd broken it. He could only hope his leg wasn't broken as well.

"Why don't you send up the doctor when he arrives, Baxter?" his mother asked. "I'll see to your father."

"Of course." He went down the stairs and found Violet pacing the drawing room, wringing her hands before her.

"Do you think he's going to be all right?" Her eyes were dark with worry.

"I believe so. We'll know more as soon as the doctor checks him." Her worry touched him. He could see how concerned she was.

"Thank goodness you came when you did. I don't know that I would've thought to walk in the opposite direction of his usual path. You found him much quicker that way." She blinked back tears and looked aside as though to hide them.

Suddenly, she turned and reached for his hands, her expressive eyes full of sorrow and holding him firmly in place. He couldn't have pulled away even if he'd wanted to.

"Baxter, I'm so sorry. I didn't mean it. I was just frustrated and I—"

"No need to apologize." He knew he'd stiffened but couldn't do anything to stop the reaction.

"Of course, there is. I never meant to insult you. I'd be honored if you—" Her mouth gaped open as she realized what she'd been about to say. "Oh, what I mean is—"

"Violet?" Her embarrassment eased his own.

She swallowed hard, eyes wide and full of hope. "Yes?"

"Perhaps you should stop talking." He kissed her, drawing her into his arms, surprised by her soft moan.

Then she wound her arms around his neck. Her embrace was all the invitation he needed to deepen the kiss. He pressed his tongue against the seam of her lips, nearly groaning with need as she gave him entrance.

She shifted, her entire body against his. She fit perfectly in his arms, making him imagine how she'd feel in his bed. Her fingers tangled in the hair at the nape of his neck, causing desire to pool hot and heavy inside him.

He couldn't say what this spark between them was, only that it held power. The problem was that he didn't know what to do with it. He would soon be leaving.

The sound of the front door opening, followed by voices in the foyer, had Baxter releasing Violet and easing back. He cupped her cheek, reluctant to release her completely. Her soft sigh made him want to give one of his own. Instead, he squeezed her hand and strode out to speak with the doctor, the scent of violets following him.

Chapter Nine

Baxter sat by his father in the small sitting room where he rested the following afternoon, Violet at his side. The doctor had declared his ankle sprained and his arm fractured. The bump to his head was concerning but not dangerous. However, the doctor suggested someone remain with him at all times to make certain his condition didn't worsen.

His father, being the stubborn man he was, refused to remain in bed. Baxter's mother had suggested a compromise by making him as comfortable as possible in the small sitting room near their connecting bedrooms. She was in the kitchen, planning his father's favorite meal with Mrs. Watsford.

"Are you warm enough, Mr. Adley?" Violet asked.

"Another log on the fire would be welcome." He sat in an armchair, supported by pillows and covered by a blanket, his bound arm in a sling. His foot had been wrapped tight and was propped on a cushioned stool.

"Excellent idea." Baxter rose to comply, pleased to do anything that might aid his recovery.

The doctor had given his father laudanum for his pain. The bottle sat on the narrow side table beside his father's chair.

Before Baxter returned to his seat, his father's soft snores filled the air.

Violet reached over to pat Baxter's arm, the gesture pleasing him. "Sleep is the best thing for him, don't you think?"

"I suppose it is." He leaned forward to touch his father's hand. "He seems chilled."

Violet rose and with careful movements, eased the blanket over the top of him.

Baxter swallowed back the sudden pressure in his chest at her gentleness. Her affection for his father couldn't be denied, and Baxter knew the feeling was mutual.

How wonderful that this woman lived next door to his parents and had reached out to befriend them when they appeared to be in need of help. Few people would've bothered.

He tore his gaze from her to look at something else—anything else—so she wouldn't guess his thoughts. He wasn't prepared to reveal them. Not when his next few years would be spent in Bombay.

His gaze fell on a book on the narrow table beside his chair, hoping for a distraction from the sudden tumult of emotions.

"What is this?" he asked, keeping his voice low so as not to wake his father.

"*The Seven Curses of London*. Have you heard of it?" Violet took the seat beside him again. She turned the cover of the book to face him. "The author lists the seven worst problems he thinks plague London."

"Is this one of the books you're reading to my mother and

father?" He could hardly believe it to be true. They had never taken much of an interest in such things.

"I mentioned it to them, and they were quite intrigued." She ran a hand over the leather cover. "It's not light reading, so we only read a few pages at a time. Otherwise, the topics tend to be rather depressing."

He opened it and turned several pages. "Neglected children. Professional beggars. Those are weighty issues."

"Your father seemed especially interested in the chapter on professional thieves."

Baxter knew why all too well.

"The author shares several viewpoints as well as firsthand accounts," Violet continued. "He also discusses the laws in place to address the issues, most of which fall short."

"Fascinating."

"In a terrible way, yes."

"How did you come to know of this book?" Ladies of her age were normally worried about what gown to wear to the next ball rather than social issues. She was even more special than he'd realized.

A smile graced her lips, causing his heartbeat to speed. "It began with my eldest sister, Letitia. She thought she was destined for spinsterhood, so took it upon herself to find a purpose for her life. She decided to help neglected children."

"That's an unusual choice for a young lady."

Violet chuckled. "You should hear her husband tell the story. It's very entertaining."

She told him a few of the events, the stories amusing despite the weighty problem.

"No wonder my mother and father were interested in learning more, though I'm certain not all of the situations were humorous."

"True. Lettie and her husband, Nathaniel, continue to help others. They've set a good example for their friends as well, many of whom have followed the same path." A pensive look came over Violet, though Baxter wasn't certain of the cause.

He asked several more questions, but she didn't reveal the reason for that look. If he hadn't been worried about his father, he might've pressed harder to find the reason for Violet's disquiet.

When his father stirred, they paused their conversation to watch him.

His lids fluttered open and caught on the pair of them. "Baxter, I'm so pleased you're spending Christmas with us."

"As am I," Baxter replied.

"And I have to say that I'm relieved you didn't marry Lady Alice."

Baxter frowned, confused as to why he'd say such a thing. He'd mentioned to his parents that he'd seen her at the ball, but his father hadn't commented on it then. "Lady Alice?" Had the laudanum addled his mind?

"I didn't care for her," he murmured, his eyes closing again.

Before Baxter could think of how to respond, his father's even breathing suggested he'd dozed off again.

Baxter cleared his throat, uncomfortable with the topic, but it didn't alleviate the tension he felt. "Lady Alice was an acquaintance of mine before I left for India."

"Was?"

Surprised at the question, he looked at her.

Pink filled her cheeks as her lashes swept down to hide her eyes. "I saw you speaking with her at the party the other evening."

"Yes." But he didn't say anything more. Alice had made her renewed interest in him clear, but he had no desire to reclaim what he'd lost. He'd already decided that when the time came to marry, he'd look for a wife who could provide connections to aid his business interests, rather than a love match, as he didn't care to risk being hurt again.

Somehow, sitting next to Violet made that idea seem a terrible one.

TWO DAYS LATER, VIOLET DONNED HER CLOAK IN HER home's foyer, prepared to walk over to the Adleys.

"You're not going next door again, are you?" Holly asked with a frown as she came down the stairs, one hand trailing along the rail.

"Yes, I am."

"What on earth do you do there all the time?"

"Yes, Violet, what do you do there?" her mother asked as she emerged from the drawing room. "It's not polite to spend as much time at their house as you do. They'll grow weary of you."

The idea that could be true hurt. Did she visit them too often? Before Baxter's arrival, she wouldn't have questioned it. But since his return, she feared her presence wasn't needed. But she enjoyed helping them and didn't want it to end. "You may remember me mentioning that Mr. Adley took a fall."

Holly scowled. "I also remember you mentioning that their son arrived from India. I wouldn't think your presence is required with him there."

Trust Holly to strike at the heart of the matter.

"Their son?" Her mother stiffened at the news. "I'd forgotten they had a son. How old is he? Violet, you cannot possibly consider him as a potential husband. He has no title, and they obviously have no funds."

Violet wanted to walk out of the house without bothering to answer. But that wouldn't help matters. How had her sisters managed to do what they'd done with their mother watching?

"I have no intention of forming an attachment with Baxter." She had to hope that Holly didn't notice the blush in her cheeks. How could Violet not blush when speaking of him brought to mind the kisses they'd shared? If she were honest with herself, she'd admit she was quite enamored with him.

"Baxter Adley." Her mother said his name as she tapped a finger against her lips, a sign she was trying to remember something.

Oh dear.

"I should be going. They're expecting me." Though they weren't.

"Wait. Baxter Adley. Now I remember. I understand he and Lady Alice are renewing their acquaintance, so it's good that you're not growing fond of him."

The pain that swept through her took her by surprise. What could Baxter possibly see in Alice? The woman might be considered a beauty, but she had directed her cutting remarks at Violet and her sister, Dalia, on more than one occasion. She was mean-spirited and often petty. Violet was tempted to warn him of her poor behavior but doing so would make her no better.

"If he likes Lady Alice, then he doesn't have good taste," Holly announced with a tone of authority.

"You've never met Lady Alice," their mother pointed out.

"I've heard enough about her to know that to be true," Holly countered.

"Holly," their mother protested. "That is hardly the way a young lady should speak of others." She looked at Violet once again. "You'd be far better off spending time trying to attract a lord's notice rather than reading to the elderly couple next door."

"I'm helping them with a few things as well." Why Violet bothered to defend her actions she didn't know.

"Such as?" Holly asked, one brow raised.

Violet's gaze swung to her mother, wondering if she truly had to answer. At her mother's matching brow, Violet sighed. "They have asked me to help them plan an old-fashioned Christmas."

"Whatever for?" her mother asked.

"They miss the activities they enjoyed in their youth." At her mother's blank look, she added, "Singing carols, decorating with holly, playing snapdragon."

"Good heavens. That is a terrible game." Her mother rubbed her fingers as though remembering it all too well.

"Maybe we could plan a few family activities this year," Violet suggested.

"Your father and I are attending a supper on Christmas Eve. And on Christmas Day, we'll all have dinner at Letitia and Nathaniel's. That is more than enough activity. The rest is far too much bother."

Her words only made Violet pleased she'd be able to enjoy some of the festivities at the Adley residence. At least then she'd have the chance to celebrate a more traditional Christmas.

"I must be going," Violet said and slipped out the door before her mother could further protest.

The icy frozen streets and walkways had melted, but the chill in the air had returned. Her breath came out in little puffs of clouds, making her release several purposely just to see them.

She chuckled at her silliness as she knocked on the Adleys' door. To her surprise, Baxter opened it.

His watchful gaze swept over her face, lingering on her lips, and bringing to mind their kiss once again. The sensation that fluttered in her stomach was becoming familiar but still threw her off balance, and there was no ice underfoot on which to blame it.

"Good day, Violet." His deep voice added to the fluttering sensation.

Oh dear. She was growing quite enamored with Baxter no matter how she wished otherwise.

THE NEXT AFTERNOON, VIOLET COULDN'T HELP BUT SMILE as she watched Baxter.

He stared at the bowl of cranberries, along with a needle and thread beside it, a look of consternation on his face. "What is the purpose of this?"

Violet giggled at his expression. "To decorate with. Don't tell me you've never threaded cranberries before."

"I can't say that I have. Have you?" he asked.

"No," she admitted. "I only said that, so it would sound like something one should do for the holidays."

"How did this idea come to mind?"

"My father's cousin lives in America and sent an entire crate of cranberries to us. My mother has no idea what to do with them. I mentioned it to my friend, Lillian, and she said the Americans often thread them on a string for decoration on the Christmas tree."

"Hmm. It seems like an odd tradition."

"Not if you don't have anything else with which to decorate."

"Don't evergreens provide enough decoration?"

"Adding a touch of red makes everything more festive," Violet advised. She gave him a pointed look. "You did say you were going to help, right?"

"I didn't realize it would involve a needle and thread."

"I promise not to tell a soul."

Baxter appeared less than impressed with her pledge. Then to her surprise, he picked up the needle.

"Be sure to tie a knot at the end of the thread first."

He did as she suggested then selected a cranberry from the bowl.

For some reason, the small gesture of him helping her string the cranberries sent her heart pounding madly. She knew he did it for his parents and not her, but her heart didn't seem to care. She bit her lip, realizing that with each day that passed, her feelings for Baxter were growing by leaps and bounds.

But he'd soon be leaving. The idea of not seeing him each day hurt already.

※

A SHORT TIME LATER, BAXTER LINGERED IN THE DOORWAY of the small sitting room near his parents' bedrooms, listening as Violet read *A Christmas Carol* by Charles Dickens to them. Her enthusiasm for the tale was apparent in the cadence of her voice. It was a far more entertaining story rather than the Seven Curses book. She even changed her tone for the various characters, making it a delight to listen to her performance.

He'd been passing through the foyer the previous day when she'd knocked on the front door. When he'd opened it, she'd been laughing. He still wanted to know why. The joy in her expression was something he wished he could imprint on his mind to pull out later when he was alone in Bombay.

Earlier, when they'd strung the cranberries on the thread, a task he would've refused to do without her at his side, he'd dearly wanted to toss aside the red berries in favor of kissing her again. No matter what they were doing, he enjoyed spending time with her.

Her joy and honesty were refreshing in an age where others tended to hide not only their intent but any hint of happiness. Ennui tended to be preferable and more fashionable.

Not for Violet.

Now, as he listened to her share an exciting scene, he couldn't bring himself to join them. He feared his growing feelings for her would be obvious to not only his parents but Violet as well. That would be disastrous.

Though she'd apologized for declaring he was the last person she'd consider as a suitor, he couldn't remove the words from his mind. For all he knew, that could very well be how she felt. Perhaps her true feelings had slipped out when she'd been speaking with her friend.

But how did that explain her response to the kisses they'd shared? Even thinking of them heated his blood.

He suddenly realized the sitting room had fallen silent. A rustle of fabric caught his notice a moment too late.

"Baxter?" Violet whispered as she appeared in the doorway. "What are you doing out here?"

"I was passing by and paused to listen." The lie came readily to his lips. Did she believe it? He hoped so as he certainly didn't want to share the truth. That he was becoming entranced by her.

"Your father fell asleep." She gestured toward the sitting room.

He nodded.

"Your mother is going to sit with him until he wakes."

"Good." Which left him with nothing more to say. He gestured for her to precede him down the hall as he searched his mind for something to fill the awkward silence. "Did you find somewhere to gather evergreen boughs and holly?"

"No, unfortunately not."

"I believe I've found a way to do so."

"That's wonderful." The happiness shining in her eyes made him feel as if he'd conquered a mountain. "Could we gather it the day before Christmas Eve? That way it will still be fresh when we decorate."

"Do you really hold to the nonsense of it being bad luck to bring greenery in the house prior to Christmas Eve?"

"Who am I to question traditions?" She smiled. "I'm going to find Watsford and request tea for your mother."

He nodded, watching as she walked down the hall, wondering again how he was going to survive when he returned to the loneliness of Bombay.

Chapter Ten

Violet dressed in her warmest wool dress and donned her heaviest stockings two days later. She'd even asked Ruth, her maid, to find the muff she hadn't worn in several years.

Not only had Baxter found a place to gather evergreens, but they were also doing so with a group. It sounded like the perfect outing for the cold winter's day. Christmas Eve would arrive tomorrow, and the decorating would begin.

And Baxter would be gone soon after.

She swallowed hard at the thought, determined to enjoy the little time she had left with him. Besides, there was so much for which to be grateful.

Mr. Adley was feeling better each day to everyone's delight. His mobility was limited, but he was in fine spirits. His excitement over Christmas was much like that of a young boy. That made Violet even more determined to make the holiday special. She had several decorations prepared, but none of it would be complete without some evergreens and holly.

Her stockings and boots should help keep her warm,

along with a felt hat. She heard the doorbell chime from her bedroom and grabbed her muff and hooded cape to hurry downstairs.

Baxter stepped into the foyer as the footman closed the door. "Good afternoon. Are you ready for our outing?"

"I believe I am, though I'm still not certain where we're going."

He only smiled as he escorted her to the carriage he'd rented. "We'll collect Viscount Beaumont and his niece and nephew then continue to where we'll gather the greenery."

"Wonderful." She didn't insist on knowing their destination. She rather enjoyed surprises. "I've met the viscount before, but what fun to have the children along."

Baxter smiled. "I didn't think you'd mind their company. He's doing his best to keep them entertained until he finds a suitable governess."

"That's no easy task. Are you certain you don't want to tell me where we're going?" She might enjoy surprises, but she couldn't help but ask. "A hint, perhaps?"

"You'll learn it soon enough." The smile on his face along with the teasing glint in his eyes was enough to cause her heart to stammer.

Why couldn't she remember that he'd soon be leaving? She bit her lip, reminding herself to simply enjoy the day.

They soon joined Viscount Beaumont along with his young niece and nephew in his coach, hot coals at their feet to warm them.

"Do you think it might snow?" the young boy asked, nearly bouncing in excitement.

"We will hope not," Viscount Beaumont answered.

But as they made their way to the outskirts of London, large flakes started to fall. The children were nearly delirious with joy at the sight.

Violet looked out the window, puzzled by the passing

scenery. "We're nearing the Duke of Burbridge's estate, aren't we?" She glanced at Baxter to find him smiling.

"That is exactly where we're going. I ran into him not long ago, and the topic of Christmas arose. When I mentioned we were in need of holly and boughs, he invited us to join the fun."

Violet chuckled, pleased at the idea. "I assume my friend, Lillian, will be there as well?"

"I believe she will."

Violet grinned. That made the day even more perfect.

In short order, she'd hugged Lillian and greeted the duke along with the others joining them—over a dozen in all. They clambered into two wagons and ventured through the snow-covered fields toward the woods. The snowflakes continued intermittently, lending a festive atmosphere as they stuck to the ground.

"I like him," Lillian whispered. "I think you should reconsider your answer to my question."

Warmth flooded Violet. Before she could respond, they were interrupted by the others.

"Will there be holly?" Viscount Beaumont's niece asked the duke as she moved to sit beside him. "And mistletoe?"

"Of course," said Burbridge. "What would Christmas be without those?"

Once they reached the area, they exited the wagons. The duke handed out several small saws as well as an axe or two and they were off, spreading out into the woods.

The day was absolutely perfect, Violet decided as she walked beside Baxter. With her hand tucked in the crook of his arm, she sighed with delight, tipping her face up to catch snowflakes. It felt glorious. "This is perfect. Well done."

"She says with a touch of surprise." He grinned at her.

She couldn't help but laugh. "I admit it. Once again, you've surprised me. I didn't expect you to be such an excellent dance partner, and I certainly didn't expect you to want to join this kind of outing. I feared we'd be climbing the neighbor's tree to cut a few boughs."

"I'm pleased you're enjoying it." His gaze searched the trees as they walked. "Do I see a hint of red berries over there?" he asked as he pointed.

"Yes!" Violet rushed forward, dragging Baxter along with her. "We must hurry before the others see the spot."

"I wasn't aware this was a competition."

"Of course it is," she said with a laugh.

Baxter climbed up the tree branches and clipped some holly, tossing it gently down to Violet who caught it in her arms. They moved to another tree to cut several evergreen boughs as well. Occasional shouts from the other members of the party could be heard, but none of their friends were in sight.

Baxter seemed to be enjoying himself despite his initial reluctance to plan Christmas for his parents. As he cut more branches, she called out, "I think we have more than enough."

"You'll need a few for your house too, won't you?"

The pleasure that filled her at his thoughtfulness had her sighing with longing.

When he'd cut more and had to pile them to the side as Violet's arms were overflowing, she laughed. "Enough," she ordered. "We'll never make it back to the wagon."

He chuckled in response as he climbed down only to lose his footing in the damp moss on the ground, falling onto his back.

"Oh dear," Violet said as she dropped the armful of branches to rush toward him. "Are you all right?"

He laid there laughing. "Yes, yes."

"Here." She offered him her hand, shaking her head at his behavior. "I'll help you up."

Before she knew what he was about, he pulled her down on top of him. "Baxter!"

His laughter faded as his gaze captured hers. "Violet." He said her name softly, as both an answer and a question layered with a pinch of promise. Placing both hands on her waist, he shifted her to fit more firmly against him.

The intimacy of the moment shocked her, stealing her breath. His gaze swung from her eyes to her lips and back again. Yes, she thought. I want that too. At that moment, she decided to seize it.

She lowered her lips to his. His mouth was warm against hers. She no longer felt the cold. Instead, a delicious heat filled her from head to toe.

His gloved hands roamed over her form. Though layers and layers of clothing separated them, she imagined those strong hands bare and moving over her. Heat pooled low in her belly, giving her the urge to shift against him.

"Miss Fairchild? Adley." The sound of a male voice calling for them broke the kiss.

But rather than shift away, Baxter pulled her tighter against him in an embrace, squeezing her heart. "I suppose we must rise and join the others."

The rumble of his words through his chest caused her breasts to tighten in the most delightful way. She wanted to remain right where she was. Not even the concern of discovery caused her to move, though she knew she should.

But at last, Baxter eased her to one side and managed to rise, lifting her upright with him. His heated gaze held on her before he straightened her cape and brushed the snow and moss from it. He turned her in a circle and did the same to the other sides of her.

With a smile, Violet returned the favor. To her surprise, Baxter kissed her again, lingering before he drew back.

"Adley, where are you?" called the voice again.

"Here we are," Baxter shouted to whoever searched for them. "Ready?" he asked her.

It took all of her wherewithal to nod, but she didn't dare say a word for fear it would be a refusal. She wanted to stay right where she was, in the circle of Baxter's arms with his lips upon hers.

BAXTER WATCHED VIOLET AS THEY ALL ENJOYED HOT chocolate, tea, cake, biscuits, and a selection of sandwiches in the duke's drawing room. A fire burned cheerfully in the hearth and spirits were high as they shared stories from the outing.

Beaumont's young niece and nephew were playing in the nursery with a maid. No doubt they'd sleep soundly on the drive back to London.

Beaumont moved to stand near Baxter. "You look as if you want to have her for lunch and perhaps supper as well."

Baxter frowned. He didn't care to think his feelings for Violet were so obvious. "She's been a true blessing to my parents."

"Nothing wrong with a little dalliance before you return to Bombay. Just don't do more than that. Our friends are dropping like flies on dung into marriage."

Baxter stared at his friend. "That's a terrible way to put it."

Beaumont lifted a casual shoulder. "I don't see the advantage of tying the knot." He tugged at his cravat as if the thought of it was enough to make him choke. "We're far too young to worry about families and the like. We deserve to have a bit of fun first."

"Says the man with two young children to raise." Baxter couldn't help but remind him.

"Yes, well, I'm in the process of searching for a governess so I can ship the lot of them to the country."

"Your niece and nephew are delightful, well-behaved children. I can see how much they already mean to you, regardless of whether you want to admit it."

"I don't know how to raise them properly. I'm the worst person to do so, and I set a poor example. But they never seem to behave for the servants. Which is why I'm in search of the right governess. More difficult to find than you'd expect."

"I can understand that you need a way to direct their energy, but don't send them away. They lost their parents and need you." Baxter should think that was obvious.

Beaumont only shook his head. "They'll be better off if they only see me at holidays."

Odd, but he didn't seem pleased by the idea.

As the afternoon began to wane, everyone made the preparations to leave. The ride back to London was quiet, the young ones sleeping soundly on the drive.

They dropped off Viscount Beaumont and the children, the viscount insisting they continue to their homes in his coach. Though his friend might protest his unexpected burden, he was gentle with his niece and nephew. Baxter hoped he changed his mind about sending the children to the country with a governess. Beaumont needed them as much as they needed him from what Baxter could see.

Baxter took the liberty of bringing Violet close to him on the tufted bench as they drove the short distance to their houses. She settled against him, and it felt as if she belonged there.

When the coach drew to a halt, he asked, "Would you come inside before you return home?"

"Only for a moment. My family will be expecting me."

He assisted her to alight, and they entered his house. All

was quiet in the drawing room, though a bright fire warmed the room. "Mother and Father must be upstairs," he said.

"I'm sure the stairs are still difficult for your father."

"I wanted to show you what I brought back from India for Mother for Christmas." He withdrew a small box from behind a large vase on one of the shelves and handed it to her.

"What is it?" she asked. At his nod, she lifted the lid and moved aside the tissue nestled inside. With careful movements, she drew the crystal piece from the box. "It's beautiful. She'll have her own Christmas star."

Baxter stiffened. He hadn't thought of the design as being a star. But Violet was right. It looked much like the Christmas star he'd wished on so many weeks ago.

For a life as big and bright and as full of hope and joy as the star.

As he stared into Violet's lovely blue eyes, he had to wonder if his wish might be coming true in an unexpected way.

Chapter Eleven

The Stavertons' holiday ball was that same night, the evening before Christmas Eve, and Violet had been looking forward to it for weeks. Even more so now that she knew Baxter would be in attendance.

She should be tired after their outing to gather evergreens but with her heart singing, how could she be? She loved that Baxter had shown her his gift for his mother. Somehow, she felt like his doing so meant something special.

After dressing in a new gown, a rich green that spoke of Christmas, she considered her appearance in the mirror, hoping she looked her best. She adored the needlework on the bodice of the gown and couldn't resist running a finger over the intricate stitches.

She knew Baxter wouldn't be at her side the entire evening. Far from it. He had many others to speak with and friends he hadn't seen since he'd left for India. Spending too much time with her would only create gossip. But with luck, she'd dance with him again. She tingled with excitement at the idea.

Tomorrow, they'd decorate his parents' home. His father

was feeling well enough that he was planning to spend the day downstairs. She intended to ask him to join in the fun by helping make a special bough for the mantle. He'd enjoy participating, she thought, which caused her to smile.

Yet she was also keenly aware that each day that brought Christmas closer also brought Baxter's departure closer. She could hardly bear the thought. Calling upon the Adleys after he left would be bittersweet. Yet she couldn't abandon them when they might need her most once he'd gone.

She closed her eyes and drew a deep breath, hoping to shove aside the worries and bury them for a few more days. Worrying over what was to come wouldn't make it go away. Enjoying the time she had with Baxter was all she could do.

With her cloak over her arm, she descended the stairs and entered the drawing room to find her father waiting, a drink in hand and a smile on his still handsome face.

"Good evening, Father." She moved forward to kiss his cheek.

"Don't you look lovely, Violet?" He set aside his glass and took both her hands. "You are an embodiment of Christmas cheer."

Compliments from her father always made her feel special. "Thank you. May I say how very handsome you look this evening?"

He executed a bow in his black suit and white shirt, his smile hinting at the rogue he must've been in his younger days.

"Are we ready?" her mother asked as she came into the room. She frowned at Violet's dress. "Are you certain that gown is a wise choice for the evening? It is very...green."

Hurt stabbed at Violet, but she reminded herself that her mother rarely liked anything her daughters wore. "I think it's quite festive."

Her mother looked resigned if doubtful. "If you insist."

Not for the first time, Violet wished her mother was more accepting of others. She knew Lettie had struggled with the lack of approval as well.

"We should go, shouldn't we?" Violet asked as she looked at her father.

He winked at her and offered his arm. They were soon in the carriage and drawing to a halt before the Stavertons' mansion. Candles glowed in all the windows, and the front door was festooned in greenery.

After greeting their hosts, her father went in one direction, her mother another, leaving Violet searching for support. She knew Lillian would be here and looked for her. It was moments like this when she was reminded of her lack of courage. Standing alone in her green dress, she felt uncertain and vulnerable. She was used to being near her older sisters or friends, but none were in sight this evening.

With a deep breath, she focused on not giving in to the desire to find a wall to hover by. She lifted her chin, determined to be brave.

"Miss Fairchild," Lady Alice greeted her as she came to stand beside her.

Of all people to speak to her, why did it have to be Alice? Was this some kind of test? Violet forced a smile, determined to take the higher road. "Enjoying the ball?"

"I am." Alice's gaze skimmed Violet's gown, a puzzled look on her face as though she was amused.

"Good evening, ladies." Baxter's deep voice had never sounded better to Violet.

He looked especially handsome this evening, his dark hair a bit longer than it had been upon his arrival, his green eyes as entrancing as ever. That gaze shifted from her to hold briefly on Alice then back again. "You look lovely this evening, Violet."

"Thank you." She wanted to reach for his arm, knowing

his touch would ease her nerves. Instead, she settled for a genuine smile, hoping he would appreciate it.

"Baxter." Alice held out her hand, expecting him to take it.

Which of course he did. It was the polite thing to do. No need for Violet to feel a sharp pang of envy just because Alice was doing the very thing Violet longed to do. Suddenly, smiling felt terribly ineffective.

"It's so good to see you again." The light in Alice's expression suggested she was very pleased.

That had Violet biting her lip. Alice was truly an attractive woman and confident. So confident that she stepped close to him, effectively cutting off Violet.

"I wanted to speak with you for a moment," Alice said, drawing Baxter forward. "In private."

"Will you excuse us for a moment?" he asked Violet.

Violet nodded, drawing a deep breath as the pair walked away. A few moments later, she saw them on the dance floor.

In that instant, Violet realized she hadn't learned anything over the past few weeks. She might have found a temporary purpose by assisting the Adleys but nothing more. They didn't truly need her. Had never needed her. Nor did Baxter.

She was still the same person who lacked the courage to take action. She'd just allowed Alice to walk away with Baxter without so much as a protest.

The realization stung. Painfully so.

Yet fighting for his attention seemed like the wrong path. If Alice was who he wanted, if she was the person who'd truly make him happy, then Violet would wish them well and step away from him and his family.

He deserved happiness. She knew how much he'd sacrificed when he'd left behind everything familiar to start a business in India. Snippets from his parents, as well as Baxter, had revealed that. Happiness seemed a fitting payment. But it wasn't in her power to provide it.

All she could do was stay out of his way. The last thing she wanted was for him to feel uncomfortable because she insisted on seeing through with her ridiculous plans for Christmas.

The lump in her throat had her swallowing hard. She glanced down at her gown, wondering if for once her mother was right and it *was* too much.

How she wished Lillian or Lettie or one of her other sisters were here. A glance about showed Baxter and Alice still on the dance floor, their steps matching perfectly. Baxter smiled, bending his head toward Alice as though wanting to catch every word she uttered. They looked like an ideal couple together.

With a shuddering breath, she turned away, her hopes for what might have been dashed. She shook her head, needing to be honest with herself. Far more than her hopes were damaged—her heart was broken. Staying here to watch the scene unfold served no purpose.

With quick steps, she found a passing servant and asked him to tell her mother that she wasn't feeling well and had returned home.

In short order, she sat in the cold carriage, alone, wishing things had turned out differently. The pieces of her heart felt jagged and painful, and she knew beyond a doubt that they wouldn't ever fit back together again.

***

"I HAD TO ASK IF IT WAS TRUE," ALICE SAID AS THEY turned on the dance floor, one brow raised, an excited light in her eyes.

"What might that be?" he asked with some trepidation.

Anything that had Alice this animated couldn't be good. He'd thought to answer her question and return to Violet's side, but she'd walked directly to the dance floor.

"That your business has attracted the interest of Bertie," she continued. Ah. That explained her excitement. Her obvious interest didn't change the realization that he no longer cared for her or what she thought.

"Prince Edward had an interest in a few things I was able to acquire for him." In fact, the prince's attention and influence had opened a new path to Baxter's business he hadn't anticipated. One that might allow him to continue the import side from London rather than living in Bombay, based on the message that had been waiting for him upon his return home from his outing with Violet. There were still many details to consider, but the opportunity held great promise.

Not that he intended to share any of that with Alice. The only people he wanted to tell, once his plans became clear, were his parents and Violet. But he didn't want to get their hopes up yet.

Alice smiled knowingly, as though she suspected him of being modest. She shifted closer as they spun, her body bumping deliberately against his, something that would no doubt start gossip if the wrong person saw it.

He refused to become entangled in her snare, so he just as quickly drew back, stiffening his arms so she couldn't repeat the move.

Anxious to return to Violet, he searched the edges of the dance floor for her, hoping she waited for him, but he couldn't see her from where they danced.

"I was sorry to hear your father has taken ill." The small smile on Alice's lips disturbed him. "I do hope he'll recover."

Baxter didn't appreciate her tone. Somehow it suggested that she hoped quite the opposite. He well remembered his father had told him that he didn't care for her.

"Actually, he's expected to make a full recovery as he merely slipped on the ice."

Her smile slid into what looked suspiciously like a scowl. "I do hope now that you've returned, we can renew our...relationship." She eased her thumb against his palm in a suggestive manner.

Why did the gesture make him feel dirty rather than desirous? Did she think that he didn't see through her interest in him now that he had money and the attention of the prince?

As Baxter took the next turn with Alice, he realized he didn't admire the color of her eyes—they were completely the wrong shade of blue—nor the way she looked at others—as though they were beneath her. What had he ever seen in her?

He made an unexpected turn, swinging her toward the edge of the dance floor. "I'm afraid I just remembered something to which I must attend."

Indeed. He'd remembered the fact that he'd rather dance with Violet.

"What?" Alice's obvious displeasure confirmed his feelings. She was not for him.

"I'm not interested in renewing our relationship. Our lives have taken different paths, but please know that I wish you happiness." He kept himself from adding that he didn't think she'd find it.

He only wanted to focus on his own. He walked away, in search of Violet, only to realize she was nowhere to be found.

***

THE NEXT MORNING, BAXTER STUDIED THE PILE OF greenery Samuel had brought into the drawing room ready to be hung. He'd expected Violet to have arrived by now. He hoped all was well, but with each minute that passed, he felt certain it wasn't.

He'd been disappointed when he'd realized she left the ball the previous evening, but knowing he'd be with her today had taken the sting out of it.

Where could she be?

A knock on the front door made him smile. He strode toward the foyer but didn't hear her feminine tones. Watsford closed the door, a message in hand.

"Was that Miss Fairchild's footman?" Baxter asked.

"Indeed, sir. He's delivered a message for your mother."

"I'll take it to her." Baxter resisted the temptation to open it himself and hurried up the stairs to where she and his father sat in the sitting room.

He waited impatiently for his mother to read it.

"Violet sends her apologies but is feeling under the weather. She won't be joining us."

Disappointment speared through Baxter. "She seemed fine at the ball." Though he supposed that would explain her abrupt departure.

"How disappointing," his father said. "She's going to miss the festivities she worked so hard to plan."

Something struck Baxter as wrong. Terribly wrong. But he could hardly march over to her house and demand to see her, regardless of whether she was ill.

As the day dragged on, he considered doing just that. He, Watsford, and Samuel hung some of the evergreen boughs for the sake of his parents, but he lacked Violet's vision for the task. In truth, he detested doing it without her as it only made him miss her more. They brought in the small tree and set it in front of the window, but he couldn't bring himself to hang the strands of cranberries on it.

Nothing was right without her.

His mother and father joined him, declaring their efforts a

success. Yet even their spirits seemed dimmed by Violet's absence.

That left him no choice. He donned his coat and hat then strode to the Fairchild's residence and knocked on the door.

"Miss Violet Fairchild, please," Baxter said and handed him his card.

The footman walked away, leaving Baxter to wait in the empty drawing room. To his surprise, not one item in the room suggested it was Christmas Eve. No greenery, no holly, and certainly no mistletoe.

A girl hesitated in the doorway, a young version of Violet with slightly sharper, gangly edges. "Are you Mr. Adley?" she asked. "Mr. Baxter Adley?"

"Yes, I am. I've come to call on Miss Violet Fairchild."

"I'm her sister, Holly." The young girl scowled as she studied him. "She *says* she's not feeling well."

Did that mean she was truly ill? Yet something in the way Holly had emphasized "says" had him hesitating. "I'm sorry to hear that. We were expecting her to call upon us this afternoon." He hoped Holly understood his meaning.

"She came home from the ball early last evening, terribly upset."

"Oh?" Baxter frowned. "Do you know why?"

"She mentioned Lady Alice was in attendance."

His thoughts caught on the moment he'd stepped away with Alice, leaving Violet alone. How stupid of him. He should've understood how that made Violet feel.

A churning ball formed in the pit of his stomach. He should've realized how his allowing Alice to draw him to the dance floor would've looked to Violet. But he thought she understood he'd return. How he wished he'd asked her to wait for him. A terrible sinking feeling formed in the pit of his stomach. Had Violet thought he'd chosen Alice over her?

Oh no.

"I need to speak with her," Baxter said. "It's imperative that I do."

The scowl returned to Holly's face. "I don't believe *I* can do anything to help with that."

He searched for her meaning. Obviously, Holly wanted to help, but her loyalty remained with her sister. "Could *I* assist in some manner?"

"Possibly." Her pleased expression suggested he was on the right path.

What he really wanted to do was march upstairs and knock on Violet's door rather than play this game. As that wasn't possible, what could he do?

She glanced over her shoulder again as though wanting to be certain she wouldn't be caught speaking to him. "It might take a gesture of some sort to convince her to listen to you."

He opened his mouth to ask what that might mean only to hear a voice call her name. "Holly?"

Her eyes went wide. "I must go." She hurried out before he could utter another word.

His thoughts raced as he considered her advice. Gesture? Of what sort? For what purpose? His thoughts whirled, unable to latch onto any answers.

The footman returned, expressing Violet's apologies but she wasn't receiving. Within a few minutes, he was walking back to his house, determined to find a way to convince Violet that he wanted her—that he cared for her and no one else.

Chapter Twelve

As evening fell, Violet sighed with frustration. What on earth was wrong with her? She was acting like a ninny. Yes, Baxter deserved to be happy. But she couldn't move past the idea that Alice would never make him so.

Why should she just step aside without giving Baxter a reason to choose her? Perhaps he didn't care for her the way she cared for him, but he had to have felt *something* when they'd kissed.

She knew one thing for certain—if she stayed in her room, she'd never know. She hadn't yet told him how she felt. Until she was brave enough to do so, she wouldn't discover what he thought of her.

Besides, it was Christmas Eve. The idea of missing out on all she'd planned for Mr. and Mrs. Adley held no appeal. She wanted to feel the burn of playing snapdragon, to help put the finishing touches on the greenery, if they hadn't already done it without her, and sing a few carols.

But more than all those things, she wanted to spend time with Baxter.

If he cared enough to call on her, didn't that mean he at least thought of her as a friend? That was basis enough for the start of something more. Why shouldn't she venture next door, at least for a brief time?

Long enough to tell him how she felt. She swallowed hard at the thought. The idea terrified her.

Yet if she didn't find the courage to speak plainly, she might regret the missed opportunity for the rest of her life. Could she live with that?

Indecision held her frozen in place, nerves stretched taut, thoughts racing, heart hammering.

Hadn't she wished on a star a few weeks ago for something new and meaningful in her life? Fate had handed her this wonderful opportunity, and she stood here, too worried about what *might* happen to act.

Not anymore.

Before she could change her mind, she retrieved a cloak and hurried down the stairs. With luck, the Christmas celebration next door had only just begun. Her own mother and father were gone for the evening. Holly was tucked in her room with a new book. No one was here to keep her from going to the Adleys'.

Her breath hitched as she considered what she could say to Baxter to explain how much she'd grown to care for him. She opened the front door with the hope that the words would come to mind when she needed them, only to find a group of carolers on the walkway before her home.

Their voices rang clearly in the crisp evening air, their faces lit by the lanterns they carried. The sight made Violet smile as she closed the door behind her. Surely their presence was a sign she was doing the right thing.

The song was one she knew well, involving shepherds watching their sheep on a cold winter's night. But the next line they sang puzzled her. *When a Christmas star appeared?* Those weren't the right words.

Then the carolers parted, revealing Baxter standing behind them, holding the Christmas star he'd bought for his mother with a lantern underneath, lighting it brightly. His gaze held hers as he walked up the steps, the carolers' voices growing quieter as he reached her.

Her heart pounded madly as she searched his face, uncertain what to think.

"There's something I didn't tell you about this star," he said.

"Oh?"

"I wished on one like it that appeared in the sky before I left Bombay. Do you know what I wished for?"

Her throat tightened at the emotions swirling in his eyes as she shook her head.

"For a life as big and bright and as full of hope and joy as the star. I didn't know exactly what that meant until I met you, Violet. You are my star."

Shivers coursed through her at his words, and she barely noticed the carolers singing louder as they moved down the street. "Baxter." She blinked back tears. "I was coming to tell you that—" She hesitated a moment then pressed on, determined to share what was in her heart. "That I have come to care for you a great deal."

"Violet—"

"No. Wait." She shook her head, realizing that wasn't quite true. If there was ever a time she needed to find the courage to reach for what she wanted, it was now. "I love you. I know it's too soon, and that we only met a few weeks ago, but it's true." With a trembling hand, she reached up to touch his cheek. "I wished on a star as well, and I am so grateful to have found you, an even better answer to my wish than I could've imagined."

He took her hand in his and pressed a lingering kiss to the palm. "I love you too. I don't think it's too soon. The heart knows, don't you think? Time is inconsequential when it comes to love."

"But, Lady Alice—"

"Doesn't matter to me. I have no wish to pursue a relationship with her and have already told her so. You are who I want. Only you, dear Violet." He kissed her, one arm wrapped around her to draw her close.

When he eased back, Violet smiled through her tears. "I'm so happy. I had no idea something like this might happen when I befriended your parents."

"Our family is so lucky that you reached out when you did. You've been a blessing in all of our lives. Will you come home with me for the evening? To celebrate Christmas Eve? Nothing is the same without you."

"I'd love to." She took his arm, anxious to see his parents, only to see the flicker of a drape moving in the window. She knew exactly who that was. "Would it be all right if Holly joined us?"

He chuckled. "I was just going to ask you that."

"It truly is going to be a Christmas to remember, isn't it?" she asked, her heart overflowing. While she knew he'd soon be leaving, that didn't make any difference at this moment. She'd wait for him, no matter how long it took.

"Who knew that wishing upon a Christmas star would bring such joy to our lives?"

"Not me, but I'm grateful for it." She rose up to kiss him briefly then rushed back up the steps and opened the door, calling her sister's name.

Epilogue

Baxter breathed a sigh of relief as he left Mr. Fairchild's library and walked down the hall to the drawing room. It was a special evening. Epiphany. The twelfth and final day of the Christmas celebration.

He wanted this night to be one that he and Violet remembered for the rest of their lives, and now that he had her father's blessing as well as that of his parents, he was ready to take the next step. He patted his breast pocket, reassuring himself the ring was still nestled there.

His heart thundered as he entered the drawing room, pleased to find Violet and Holly there, just as her father said they'd be.

Violet smiled in surprise at his entrance as she rose from a chair. "I didn't know you were here. I didn't even hear the door."

He winked at Holly then took Violet's hands in his, not telling her that he'd arrived early to speak with her father. She'd learn that soon enough. "I was anxious to be with you." That much was true.

They'd spent as much time as possible together in the

past twelve days, and he'd fallen more in love with her each day. He couldn't wait to share what was in his heart. If he had to say it in front of Holly, he'd do so. It couldn't wait another moment.

"Violet," he began.

"Oh." Holly stood abruptly, eyes wide as she stared between them. "I just remembered that I forgot something in my room. Excuse me." The smile she gave him as she hurried past suggested she had a good idea of what he was about to say.

Was it written on his face? But when he looked back at Violet, she didn't seem to notice anything untoward.

"You are incredibly beautiful," he said.

She smiled. "You look very handsome as well."

"I have good news."

Her brows rose. "What might that be?"

"Prince Edward has made several introductions for me, involving some of the items I've been importing. Those connections are going to make it possible for me to continue my business from London."

"Truly?" Violet's eyes filled with tears, her face lit with joy. "That's wonderful news."

"I might have to travel to Bombay occasionally, but I can remain here for the most part."

"Baxter, I'm so thrilled." She squeezed his hands and started to move closer.

"Wait," he bid her, knowing that if she was nearer, he might not say all he wanted to say. "There's more."

"Oh?" Her brow furrowed as if she couldn't imagine what else he might share.

"As you know, Epiphany is the night the Christmas star brought the wise men to see Jesus. I can't imagine a better night to celebrate what a bright star I saw in Bombay brought me." His stomach clenched, his heart pounding as he lowered to one knee.

Violet's mouth dropped open, her beautiful blue eyes round with surprise.

"Would you do me the great honor of becoming my wife?"

"Yes. Yes. Yes." Her eyes overflowed, and her happy tears nearly caused him to do the same.

He reached into his pocket and withdrew the ring. The brilliant diamond was as close a match to the star as he'd wished on all those nights ago. "I love you, now and forever," he promised as he slid the ring on her finger.

"Baxter! This will be my own Christmas star." Violet wound her arms around his neck, and he rose to embrace her. "I love you as well. Forever and always."

WATCH FOR GAMBLING FOR THE GOVERNESS COMING soon! Sign up for my newsletter https://lanawilliams.net/ if you'd like to know when it releases, see a special excerpt, and be the first to hear other news.

Also by Lana Williams

Victorian Romances:

The Seven Curses of London Series

Trusting the Wolfe, a Novella, Book .5

Loving the Hawke, Book 1

Charming the Scholar, Book 2

Rescuing the Earl, Book 3

Dancing Under the Mistletoe, a Christmas Novella, Book 4

Tempting the Scoundrel, a Novella, Book 5

Falling for the Viscount, Book 6

Daring the Duke, Book 7

The Secret Trilogy

Unraveling Secrets, Book I

Passionate Secrets, Book II

Shattered Secrets, Book III

Medieval Romances:

Falling for a Knight Series

A Knight's Christmas Wish, a Novella, Book .5

A Knight's Quest, Book 1

The Vengeance Trilogy

A Vow To Keep, Book I

A Knight's Kiss, a Novella, Book 1.5

Trust In Me, Book II

Believe In Me, Book III

Contemporary Romance:

Yours for the Weekend, a novella

If you liked this book, I invite you to sign up to my newsletter to find out when the next one is released: https://lanawilliams.net/

If you enjoyed this story, please consider writing a review!

About the Author

Lana Williams is a USA Today Bestselling and Amazon All-Star author who writes historical romance filled with mystery, adventure, and a pinch of paranormal to stir things up. Filled with a love of books from an early age, Lana put pen to paper and decided happy endings were a must in any story she created.

Her latest series is The Seven Curses of London, set in Victorian times, and shares stories of men and women who attempt to battle the ills of London, and the love they find along the way that truly gives them something worth fighting for.

Her first medieval trilogy is set in England and follows heroes seeking vengeance only to find love when they least expect it. The second trilogy begins on the Scottish border and follows the second generation of the de Bremont family.

The Secret Trilogy, which shares stories set in Victorian London, follows three lords injured in an electromagnetic experiment that went terribly wrong and the women who help heal them through the power of love.

She writes in the Rocky Mountains with her husband, two growing sons, and two labs, and loves hearing from readers. Stop by her website at www.lanawilliams.net and say hello! You can also connect with her on Facebook, Twitter, Pinterest, and Instagram.